THRONE OF THE PANTHERS

DENNIS FISHER

Library of Congress Control Number: 2024921688

ISBN
978-1-964488-32-5 (Paperback)
978-1-964488-33-2 (eBook)
978-1-964488-31-8 (Hardcover)

THRONE OF THE PANTHERS

TABLE OF CONTENTS

It Begins

On the distant continent of Africa, a beautiful night has an overly abundant amount of stars. It is as if they were gathering together in this one location. The air is calm, there is nothing stirring, and the mood is somber. One can look in all directions and notice the tranquility. The peaceful scene is only marked by a huge light from a village in the distance, which would go unnoticed otherwise. A closer look into the village reveals a people in mourning. Their old king has passed on to the ancestral grounds to join his kin.

He is beloved by his people and family. For he is the "Bringer of Peace," he is the one king to take a stance and bring order to the warring tribes.

Those were bloody times; men cared not for the people, only the conquest. Their driving motivation was simply greed! What started out as wanting what was right for the different nations gave way to the desires of men. But one man remained loyal to the belief of the people. With the allegiance of multiple tribes, this one man used cunning and tactics never before seen. Only to rise as the one true king… King Lobengula! Under his leadership, many tribes rise to give birth to one prosperous nation of people.

The prosperity and structure that he instills gives the people a face, and they love him for this. He will be the first to be enshrined in the royal chamber. The construction of his pyre was a joyous occasion; the people celebrated the life of their king and mourned his death as a tribute. The newly constructed burial chamber has the king's armor, shield, sword, and royal headdress. All these are staged at a throne to honor him. It is decreed that only one of the royal bloodlines can enter the chamber and must construct the shrine to the predecessor. It is difficult for the young king. He is the first to complete this task. He is as powerful and righteous as his father, but vulnerable as his child. He is now king, King Menelek. His rule begins at the age of twenty, and a reputation for being wise and diversified in his decisions is his pedigree.

He is also known for his vision of the future. Maybe because of who he is, that this is the reason he is chosen to ignite the flame of the future?

Whatever the reason, on this night, the young king is in counsel with the kingdom's oldest and most revered elder. She is old and grizzled. Her body is small and frail. She is known for always being dressed in ceremonial garb. Her eyes show her wisdom; they are ancient and mystic. She has seen the dark days and gives a glimpse of what is to come.

It is her words that give life to what is to be. "You, young king, you are to be the father of the future of this nation. Your life's legacy will foster in a great gift to the kings to come beyond you. Hear me now, young king.

You must never waver from the path of righteousness. Your morality, wisdom, strength, honor, bravery, and knowledge must all be instilled in your descendants. For all, save one, could be chosen at any time to accept this gift. The gift will only arise from a tragedy from within. Your family must purge itself of all evil for this to prevail. That time is predestined and will not be pleasant for your family. Many must be sacrificed in order for the prophecy to come to form. Hearts will be heavy, but events will be triggered by this tragedy that will alter the course of the world!" And the night is again silent…

For a time, all rejoiced in the prophecy to come. But generations have come and pushed many to the ancestral lands as time continually ushers in life. And with new life, the old lives, ways, and traditions fade into memories, then into stories told beside fires, and finally almost forgotten fables…

CHAPTER 1

DESTINY'S VOYAGE

In the dead of night, a loud roar of thunder conspires with the deafening waves as they crash against a lone ship. The solid black wall of the night is only briefly revealed as a mighty crooked bolt of lightning streaks across the sky. The ship that is isolated in the murky giant river is only compounding the dreaded night with her creaking and twisting moans of stress from the relentless giant, never-ending river.

The loud rantings of the strangely dressed and pale being, constantly screaming at the cargo, are not only unfamiliar but also maddening. The more the people try to understand it but fail, the louder it roars! In the dark, a menacing figure can be seen walking to and fro down the corridor. And it utilizes the long leather weapon that has a brilliant flash of pain that clashes against the elders' flesh.

It is a horrifying sight. A child wants to run to the safety of his mother and grandmother, but metal restraints upon his neck along with heavy bracelets around his ankles prevent him from moving. His father is not far from the child's sight. He is a prince. Prince Girma, strong and virile. The entire village looked forward to the day that he would lead them.

Yet in the chaos of the raid, he fell. The screams of the unsuspecting village resonate across the plains. Many families had not yet risen from their peaceful slumber. Although the culprits and the purpose of the assault was unknown by unprepared victims, many brave men and women attempted to defend their homes, families and neighbors. But despite their strengths, skills and ferocity, it was as if every movement was anticipated. As if individuals were targeted, culling the strong from the more vulnerable. Blood streamed through the pathways of the village homes. Many tried to escape. Some did, but the majority did not. Women screamed and children cried, but their tears were witnessed only by the wind and the rays of the early morning sunlight. The attackers did not seek to destroy the village or it's entire people. But rather they gathered and bound them. For most of the elders, it was instant death. The trees and fields of grain swayed back and forth as if catching the newly released souls and transporting them away from this scene of devastation. An elder woman could be heard through the madness. Her last breath a single word, "Cowards." It was clear that this siege was deliberate and coordinated. As a result of men from the south surrounding his home, on that day, the boy's father gathered his weapon and shield. Once assured of his family's escape, he burst through the entrance of their shelter. They had laid in wait for him. Men on either side. Men to the front and even atop of the home of the prince. They attacked him in the blink of an eye. He never had the opportunity to act.

That was mild compared to what had transpired next. One attacker pierced his side with a spear. Another hit him with such force across the back of his head that it caused the impact of the crushing blow from the attacker to the front to split his nose and mouth! The once powerful, now limp body fell motionless to the ground! His son fears for him, but could not cry as the boy's grandmother, queen Akilah, held her hand over his mouth and drags him to an opening to the rear of the hut.

She and the boy's mother, the princess Adero, had some time ago ordered that a cut out, a small opening in the wall, be carved to allow the three to escape oppressors! The child wanted to stay and help his father, for he was the son of a prince. But nonetheless, he was still a child. His mother and grandmother knew this. So they scurry through the opening out into the tall grass. The demure grandmother moved like a lioness hunting her prey. The shock that the boy was experiencing made this all seem so surreal.

She hurries through the tall grass, into a ravine, down about 50 – 60 paces and out into the trees. She motioned for her daughter to hurry and with that, placed the child on her back. The shock of the atrocities not only affected his perception, but paralyzed him as well. None of this seemed real, as if it were a terrible dream that continued to play out.

The child prince could still hear the screams and cries from the villagers! He began to feel again, and that feeling was fear!

Without warning, he burst out with a blood-curdling scream. It had just dawned upon him, the realization of what was happening. His mother falls to the ground with him and held her hand over his mouth. It was not with the mother's touch that he was accustomed to. Her whispered but stern words quickly made him realize the danger that he may have caused! She told him, "Be Silent, or We shall all be captured or killed!" His grandmother's gentle eyes pierced his soul as she spun around as if to silence him herself. His mother commanded that he should remember that he was a prince and that he should behave as such. Cowardice was not acceptable and should not happen again. His grandmother hastened the pace… they moved against slashing branches on all sides. But she moved with purpose; she was heading to the nesting thicket. He remembers now, his father taught him these places during his training to become a man had not too long ago begun. Now he knows where they must go, so he aides in their dash for freedom by catching up to his grandmother.

Sanctuary is reached! They scuttle into the underbrush and make their way down into the earth beneath the boulders. His mother drags the boulders along the dirt slope back in place and quickly takes him into a powerful embrace. Although he welcomes her touch, it is obvious she needed his comfort more than he could have imagined. The young prince wanted to be strong for his mother and grandmother, so he devoured his fears and searched for a weapon of some type. His father had told of weapon caches throughout the jungle in all of the overnight spots. It didn't take long for him to find what was needed: food, knives, shields, and spears! Now he could defend his family and rescue his father.

As they settled in and tried to make sense of what was happening, his mother and grandmother were planning their next move and timely ascent from refuge. He moved closer to the opening, expecting the worst and preparing for anything. Out of the chaos, he hears voices and motioned for his mother to come and help him to decipher them… "Numair, Numair!" It was clear to him whose voice was calling. His heart filled with relief to hear this voice!! He attempted to drop everything and run out to him… but his grandmother held him back. Why?

Once again, she covered his mouth. Instantly, he sensed something was wrong.

His relief now gave way to fear!! His heart was racing and the blood from his veins began to boil. The fears quickly pushed aside, he gathered his wits and rearmed himself. With his spear at the ready, his knife by his side, and a shield before him, he was ready. His body tensed and lay at the ready like the giant cats before they strike. His eyes stayed focused on the opening and his ears captured every sound… but there was nothing. He listened more intently because he didn't want to let his guard down too soon. And still nothing. He looked over at his grandmother, who had eased next to him. too, was armed and ready. Her eyes showed the thoughts that the boy's mind was whispering, the danger had passed. Akilah motioned to her daughter that all was clear and began to move to the back of the overnight encampment. As she did so, her movements caused the slightest soil to fall downward. In that same instant, the boulder was plucked from the opening and boy's body reacted! The blinding light impaired his vision, so he lunges his spear forward without thinking yet focused on the area directly forward!! He hits his mark and hears the death scream of someone! Suddenly, a figure snatches the child and pulls him from their safe spot. The grasp is like metal, it crushes the prince all over. He is forced to drop the weapon and shield. He screams out… A painful reminder that he is but a child.

Gathering his vision, he is horrified to see that it is his uncle, Sammiel, that has a hold on him! He sees the loathing in his eyes for him, but why? His grandmother, Queen Akilah, is thrown to the ground by her hair and kicked in the face! His struggle to break free is in vain. His grandmother takes on yet another form!! She is behaving weak and fragile, and totally helpless. Her eyes sparkle, and so does Sammiel's! Simultaneously, he shouts to his men to move! At that very moment, his grandmother exposes her hidden blade and slits one of her captors' throats!! The uncle, with the speed of a cheetah, flings the boy to the ground where the child is quickly rounded up by other men and heel kicks the old grandmother in her face, his own mother!

"Throw them in with the rest of the lot," he shouts. He sneers at Adero and tells her that now is the time of his reign and that they all will pay for their success and pushing him to the side! What is he talking about? He and his brother did everything together! Prince Girma, the boy's father, confided with him on any and everything! Was he mad? What would turn him into this monster? In this moment, the boy didn't care. He only wants to strike back and help his family. He is rigid with terror and anger at this man whom he's known and loved all of his life. Now he doesn't know what this is before him. He is a stranger, a monster, and the disbelief is overshadowed by rage!

"No longer am I the other child, the future king's brother!" He shouts at his mother. His eyes burn with contempt, his voice roars with anger, and his eyes sear her soul with hatred! "You are mad," Princess Adero shouts.

"Why have you done this? You've turned against your own family at their hour of need. Tribes have united with our most hated enemy. Seeking our demise, and you choose now to whimper like a dog over some imagined slight?"

With the blood-curdling laugh of a Hyena, he proudly boasts, "Fool... I am the enemy... Hahahaha. You think that I am inciting a coup during an attack from a rival... hahahaha? I've joined forces as part of the new alliance between our tribes! They get a few slaves and the immediate royal family, and I begin a new era of leadership. One that is long due to me! You all can thank me, for I have their assurance of your lives being spared. Your home and land will be forever out of sight. You will be sold into bondage by men from the western lands, far across the giant rivers. You shall be the lap dogs of strangers!"

And with that, he slapped Queen Akilah to the ground! The force was so great that both her mouth and nose streamed blood. The boy's thoughts were simple: where was his father, and how could he end this madness? With that, they were restrained with metal and bound to one another by strange pale beings. They are foul-smelling and in tattered and soiled clothing. The metal was hot from the sun and pinched their skin, but it burned the very flesh that it touched. And as hard as he tried not to, the boy began to cry… after dragging and pulling them through the dense jungle, they finally came back to what remained of the village. And there, more horrors awaited them. They noticed that familiar faces had helped Sammiel in this ordeal. Some of them even spat on both the princess and queen mother!! But how could they betray their royal family? Why would they? The sight of the boy's father was the most horrifying of all. He was beaten down to a huddled mass of flesh. They could hardly recognize him, save for his scar that he bore on his left cheek. However, he no longer seemed limp and lifeless, but instead, a sense of strength in him began to rise. He caught sight of his family and motioned the group to not acknowledge him. Although young, the boy understood that now was the time to observe and gather information before making a hasty and possibly costly decision.

But that was all short-lived and seemed to be a potion-induced dream that they all share and have yet to awaken from for many days and nights. The young prince calls out to his father to hear if he is alright, but that was drowned out by the loud crack of thunder. He could hear his mother calling to him as well… "Girma, are you well?" she shouts. And the relieving response was very welcomed, "Adero, I am fine. How is everyone? Where is my mother? Where is queen Akilah?" They all respond in kind that they are fine and alive. But before they can deduce what has happened to them or where they are, the child prince feels a tearing at his flesh and hears the crackling sound of a lash!

It is another pale being, but only he seems to command respect from the others as they move to the side and follow his bellows and shouts. He takes a hard look at the boy and suddenly grabs his restraints. He pulls him up from his position and studies the child like one would look at a dressed piece of gazelle. Do they eat us? Is this why we were betrayed to satisfy their appetites? The prince's mind was filled with countless unanswered questions. The family tried to reach the prince and free him from the creature. But the results were severe lashings, kicks, and more shouting in that strange language again.

The restraints are undone at this man's command. A fat, dirty, and smelly man takes hold of the boy by the arm and tears him away from the others. As the boy felt his grip loosen, probably because he was a child, he quickly struck the man in his groin area with all of his might! He doubled up and loosened his hold on the prince. The little prince rolled over onto his back and saw other men coming towards him!! With one glance, saw his chance and slid between two of them. After a quick roll, he made it to his mother and grandmother. Only inches from them, a strange sensation came over the boy. He observed his grandmother's eyes, filled with disbelief. Suddenly, he was immobilized. He was spun around and before him stood a strange little yellow man just slightly taller than he. And with two fingers, pop, he struck the boy's neck with lightning speed and he was out. Into a deep sleep, he fell. That was the last thing that he remembered and the last time that he would see his family for some time. The events have taken a strange turn, leaving him with no recollection. It's like a bad dream. He had never witnessed such actions or speed before. His curiosity sparked questions about his identity and origins.

As the boy awoke, oh how he ached, still groggy from the fight. Where am I? How long have I been out? He wondered. He makes it to the edge of the small sleeping rig and looks around the area. It must be sleeping quarters for their captors. Just as he wheels around, he is yanked by the neck! It's the one in charge! It seems he is constantly accompanied by a group of men. The little prince waits until he notices the yellow man. Hahahaha, everyone looks as though they anticipate an attack... humorous.

The grip is painful and with intent. He is led down a small dark corridor and into a room equally dark. A small window and a burning cauldron provide the only illumination in the room. The quarters are cramped with peculiar seating arrangements. But in the corner is the yellow man! He stands so stiff, as though he were a tree. The boy is thrown his way, but for what purpose? Surprisingly, he holds the child by the arm and keeps him at bay, strange. The leader is talking to this yellow man-child, and he understands him. It is evident that he is from a different tribe. Why does he understand this language? None of that matters at the moment; for the group departs, and it is just the yellow man and the little prince. He loosens his grip and goes to the opening of the room, and looks around. He returns and gestures for the boy to come to him. That makes no sense to the boy, so he does not move. He gestures again, but with the same result. He does this again and again the child refuses, but this time... he spins and before the child knew it, he was entrapped with a strange metal rope! Numair struggles to free himself, without success. And with one pull... he stands before his overseer. The boy finds the yellow man's calmness fascinating. However, the boy possesses his own uniqueness. With a quick snap, Numair is free! The overseer has had this thing around his waist, completely unnoticeable. This is not an ordinary man! Something is different about him; an odd being, this stranger, who is not like the others. Yet he seems unnerved and quite composed. He is not a bulky adult like Numair's father or the other men of the village, he's smaller than the other captors, but they dare not approach him out of respect. A small man, he is not imposing. He is no threat to the unsuspecting, nothing to speak of to the untrained eye.

He is now the young prince's personal keeper. He takes the boy by the hand and motions for him to clean the room. He takes Numair to everything that he is supposed to attend to for the care of this room. Is this the way that they treat their captives?

The room is filthy and cluttered. The boy is led around to each area as though he were in a form of training. After several areas of cleanings, he is halted and taken out of the room. The yellow man leads him down a narrow passageway, there the wood is of foul smells with an old oily black buildup and is dimly lit. Up to the top. Here, Numair realizes they're on an immense long boat. This giant river surpasses any that Numair and his people have ever experienced. The wooden walkway is long, old, and grey. There are, what appear to be, tall leafless trees rising from the walkway. Attached to them are heavy clothes that seem to take blows from the wind. And the wind makes its presence known by dancing along the riggings of the cloth and riggings of the long boat. The enormous river appears to dance along with the wind as it hurls gigantic waves across the bow of the ship. Young Numair takes in his surroundings for a moment. It is here that the child sees his home in the distance. They're distant from land, rain relentlessly pounds through the night. He can see for the first time that this is not a terrifying dream and his world will never be the same.

The skies are dark and grey, making the long boat seem ominous. He feels as though he cannot stand up or breathe. Suddenly he is running to the edge of the longboat and throwing up. He feels dizzy and weak; he has never felt this way before. But the yellow man gathers up the boy and leads him to an area of containers. Numair sees him pick up two small containers of wood. And points to the child, then the containers and finally to the smaller containers. What an odd fellow, he hasn't said a word yet he seems to command young Numair's attention, strange.

Yet he understands what is commanded of him to do, he thinks to himself humph! I am no servant! As he begins to walk away, he is prepared for this man, or so he thought… With the speed of the wind, the little yellow man makes his presence known! However, Numair is also prepared, with some surprises of his own. As anticipated, the yellow man reaches for Numair very swiftly. But the agile young prince sidesteps his advance. With all of his strength, Numair strikes two quick blows to the chest and face area of his aggressor. That was his attempt, at least. With blinding speed, without notice, this man deflects Numair's attempts and strikes him like a viper. Once again, the boy was unable to move. With three lightning fast strikes, Numair is motionless and only able to stand watch as the crew bursts out with a roar of laughter. The boy can see the yellow man circle him, but he flows like water and, just as flawlessly as he began, he is again in his unassuming posture!

He now approaches Numair. He's in the boy's face with this stern look in his eyes, he again points to the array of containers. But this time he nods to Numair… the boy understands, but he cannot move. He stares at the little prince with an expectation of a response look. Again, there is no movement.

With a simple, unimposing gesture, one, two little pricks of his fingers, Numair again is in control of his faculties! WHO IS THIS LITTLE MAN? Although the boy is trying to find a resolution to his family's predicament, he is in awe of this man.

His family, he longs for this nightmare to end!

As he is ordered to remove the tops of the large containers, Numair discovers that it is food that he is being ordered to transport from container to container. As he begins to move food from one container to another, the little yellow man has placed a long pole beside the smaller containers.

Why? If anything, the last few encounters with this yellow man have shown Numair, is that he has a plan for him. Numair has now come to expect that from him!

The proud little prince is now reduced to a load bearer. He is humiliated, and the crew is laughing at him. The filthy gaggle of misfits, he thinks to himself!

Their garments tattered and soiled, their hair matted like that of the mad, the outcasts of the plains. Some have open wounds and dried substance throughout their bodies, a horrid sight. And he, a prince, is reduced to being their entertainment! He shall give them nothing further to cackle about! With the skill of an experienced captor, he scoops food into the smaller containers and lifts the pole with one foot at the same time and thrusts it up into his free hand. As the containers fill, he slides the pole between the lift ropes. Before the lifts can relax, he catches the pole on his shoulders and turns abruptly to the yellow man. The look of vagueness on his face was betrayed only by the approving, ever so slight nod of his head. Numair is led again down below to the cooking compartment. It is dark and illuminated only by the light of the large fire breathing metal barrel. Inside is a filthy wretch of a man. He grins and is saying something to the yellow man, who, judging from his expression, is not too fond of his taunts. At that time, the lumbering behemoth is on top of the child and pulling him by the hair. Numair has had enough of this humiliation and will no longer stand for it! With a mighty turn, he swiftly kicks his assailant directly under his mouth, just as his father had taught him. The blow caused the brute to release his hold and stagger back. As he falls, he lands against a wood bed aligned with an array of knives. In one swift motion, the giant frees a knife and recoils to strike the boy down. A figure, swift as a cobra, strikes without hesitation. In one swift moment, the yellow man has a rigid stance with his leg coiled and the giant stilled and dazed. The giant stands motionless, silent, and unwavering. Then a trickle of blood makes an appearance as it begins its descent down to his mouth, which has changed its shape, as well as his nose. Before the boy's eyes, the giant's facial features have totally transformed, and with the slight breeze from the little opening to the side. He falls. An improvement, if I do say so myself, thinks Numair. Now he is impressed.

Numair cannot conceive how this small framed man is so powerful that his enemies fall with such ease. The tiny giant slowly uncoils and gently lowers his rigid leg. Numair has never seen anyone use their body in such a manner. This man's entire body seems to be a weapon of deadly force. The more he witnesses these actions, the more Numair is in awe of this man.

But he cannot allow this to sway his purpose. For he has been shown an opportunity and must use this opportunity to his advantage. As the events leading up to this moment, he has discovered a source of food and a cache of weapons. He must not give way to temptation and act too hastily. Numair has to bide his time and act at the proper moment.

Currently, they make additional trips to gather more food. With each venture, he surveyed the area and found several passageways back to his family and his new quarters. Now, to actually have the opportunity will be the most challenging part of this plan. But it must happen; he cannot fail his family and people.

He opens his eyes to the sounds of warthogs grunting and snorting all around him. Because of his age or because his personal jailer perhaps is not concerned, but whatever the reason, Numair has freedom to move about the ship. Now is his time!

CHAPTER 2

TRANSCENDENCE

The loud sounds of sleep assure him of the freedom to carry out his intent. Numair makes his way from the crowded quarters and pulls forth the heavy wooden opening cover. It whines like a jackal in the night, but is silent against the sleeping men's horrible sounds. A dash to the opening and pause to take stock of the remaining members of this collection of miscreants.

There is one at the wheel, one on either side of the long boat, and a roamer… easy. Numair measures the cloud cover and moves with a transformed swiftness that only the royal bloodline has. He makes his way to the large containers of food and positions the smaller containers to one side. Then scampers up the large dead tree in the center and remains motionless. He scans the area and sees the roamer making his way past Numair's target and continue on. The one on the wheel and the other two sentries remain the same. They seem uninterested in their task, fortunate for the boy. He slides his way back down to the large containers. Swift are his actions, deliberate is his task. Numair gathers the two containers in one fell swoop and makes his way down again to the sleeping quarters. He knows not of a way to get the food down to the people with a sentry at the opening and more along the long wooden walkway. But there is a large caged opening that will serve his purpose. Lying flat on his stomach, Numair finds a body awake and looking directly into his eyes. He motions to her to move the food along as it comes down. They begin the coordinated plan and continue on until all have a fulfilling meal, something that has been missing for some time. They have a small victory.

They continue this ritual for about two moon cycles. Everything is a bit more tolerable at the moment.

The morning stirs as usual and Numair has his usual toils of labor. Servant to his oppressor at the break of day, the boy wakes him with a container of ale and bread. Listening to his body noise every morning has become a bit of a mark for the type of day that they will have. Loud bolstering bursts mean that the leader, who is now known as the captain, is feeling good and there will be no issues this day. But if the sounds are wet and repeating and at a rapid pace, he has had a disturbing meal and too much ale! His bloating belly is sour and upset, which is a sign that he is miserable and everyone is to pay for his discomfort. Let us hope for a happy belly. Their routine is simple, Numair feeds him, aides him in dressing, and carries his filthy night fluid bowl to be discarded from the topside of the longboat. Mornings, after their routine has been completed, the boy returns to fashion the captain's oddly soft sleeping container. It has many fabrics covering it. All heavy and warm, the nights on the giant river are cold and can be unbearable for some. When the meal is complete for him, he fancies his remains to the young, proud prince as a reward... swine! But Numair must keep appearances as the docile and humble child if he is to continue to care for the others below. Once the duties are complete, he must stand near this foul-smelling man and bring him documents of the vast giant river. Clever Numair is beginning to understand their meaning from his daily acquaintance with these parchments. Has learned to plot course from any direction of his current location. The captain takes notice of his inquisitive nature and finds it amusing, perhaps he does not believe that a child of the motherland could comprehend these parchments, let alone that the boy even knew what he was looking at. He could even believe Africans are too ignorant to have thoughts. Whatever the misguided thinking may be, Numair uses it to his advantage. After the coordinates are confirmed, Numair must put away the parchments and is then released to aid the yellow man.

The yellow man, who he now knows to be Kang, always has something for prince Numair. The boy notices that his arms and legs are enlarging and the pain that used to accompany this grueling routine no longer exists. Every day with Kang feels like an ongoing training for his manhood. He instructs the prince to certain duties topside that end up in the belly of the longboat. They repeat and increase the ritualistic chores with precision. Numair is not allowed to use ladders. He has to jump from one pole to another as he carries items to be stored on upper levels of the storage bay. This leads to lifting heavy baskets and ropes from the decking to the upper levels with long poles. In the beginning, this task was impossible to accomplish, but Kang would not allow Numair to stop. He would simply lighten the loads until the young prince could manage them. Prince Numair's arms and wrists are powerful and chiseled. He gives the prince lashings against his legs if he does not position them in the manner that Kang desires. Numair feels as if he is riding the great elephant from the plains. But time has sculptured him and his stance is solid, he feels locked to the ground beneath his feet. Finally, they end the session with rope binding. Numair now loves this the most. In the beginning, it was not so much fun. They began at either end and intertwine rope around their hands, elbows, and shoulders. As they do so, they are in their stances and must pull against one another's strength to ensure the ropes are bound tightly. As they get nearer to one another, they maneuver against one another to finish the task as a whole. Here is where it gets fun. Kang's hand gestures before greatly befuddled Numair. The young prince has studied him and learned of his secrets, now as Numair employs the same tactics upon Kang, Numair is faster and more deceptive in his moves, their hands are blurring to the naked eye, but with precision. Kang smiles, (or what appeared to be a smile It was a curvature of his mouth… disturbing), as Numair bested him on this glorious occasion. The work is effortless, and the prince is able to help his people and keep them healthy until he can find some way of freeing them. He must be careful and the missing food is being questioned. A worry that he cannot allow to let alter his objective. His father is regaining his strength, but he longs to see them all fully restored. Instead, it is simple gestures that everyone is surviving that has fueled his determination. The only possible hindrance will be the fat, grotesque figure of a man… the one who does women's work to feed the masses.

Each day, he is questioning more about the supply of food. He is suspicious, but cannot be sure. Numair must be ever so careful not to be discovered. Tonight will be a challenge indeed, for the large warthog of a man is planning something. Numair knows this from his glaring glances towards him.

He is careful not to raid the stores every night. Every other night is the time that prince Numair makes his advance. Tonight is the other night! It must be done.

But this night is different. There is something sinister about. By now, his people are aware of the routine and await the boys' arrival. But this night… this night unveils untold horrors for the people held as cargo. The young prince is halted by a shaking head and wide gaze of his young female accomplice. She is terrified and tears stream from her young eyes. Befuddled, Numair scrambles to get a glimpse of her terror. The boy is horrified! There is a small group of the crew imposing themselves upon the women and children held as cargo. In an instant, the carefree days of a life filled with innocence and love are brutally stripped away. The loving touch of a friend or loved one is cruelly replaced by pawing hands and brutal strikes. The cargo hold is filled with angry and terrifying screams of proud husbands, warriors, mothers, daughters, and defenseless people. But all for naught, as their voices go unchecked. The helpless Numair can only witness the horrifying acts. But that night burned in his memory along with other atrocious events against his people. Murders, rapes, beatings will no doubt form the mindset of this young prince. That night and others like it, have been buried deep in memories as the people and Numair are at the mercy of their captures for now. Time passes by with the mundane routine of daily work overshadowing the pain.

Tonight the giant river is angry and tosses the long boat all about. Huge walls of water engulf the sides of the long boat. The men are thrown about like shreds of thrashed grain. They are clumsy and occupied. Numair waits longer than usual to advance up top. He can sense that a plan has been set in motion, but to no avail. Numair has already set stores in another location from his daily duties. All that is needed now is to take it to them and pass them down.

As the hour grows late, the storm is stronger. He hears adult men screaming and loud scuttle noise from all over the long boat, they are in total disarray. Now is his opportunity! He must move with purpose, swift and deliberate. He rounds the upper deck entrance to a small cubby and retrieves his cargo, now to get to the opening and begin the process of feeding without discovery, a task not quite inviting.

As he moves towards the tall leafless trees in the center of the vessel, he can sense someone. Without a thought, he whirls as though he is just as disoriented as his captors and tosses his cargo into a corner with one motion.

Not to his surprise, it is the warthog, standing with his back to him from the left. He hasn't seen the boy, but that is only temporary. As Numair regains his composure, still mimicking his captors, he spins to find the prince in his sights. He moves towards Numair and takes a long hard look, as if searching for something. With no such findings, he flings the prince to one of the filthy. He searches, but finds nothing. Could it be because he's too stupid to actually look for the stolen goods? It's not but a few steps from him when he turns and begins to shout. As he does, another filthy one runs to the now gathered group. Their faces change. They all rush together like a herd and scurry down below. Silly oafs, they had the perfect opportunity to catch Numair. He cannot help but to laugh at these twits. He waits for them all to leave, he has but a few brief moments to have the topside to himself. A brief survey of his surroundings and he is alone. This is just perfect. He could not have planned this any better, the cover of darkness and no one around to impede his purpose.

Now's his chance, without a moment's hesitation, Numair gathers his belongings and heads towards the opening. What is witnessed horrifies him!

The area below was submerging in water! He could see some people still in their positions, floating beneath the water, their eyes open! Panic-stricken, he rushed to them and disregarded his cargo. His only thoughts were of his family. Just as he reached the opening, an iron hand clasped his shoulders and held him still, it was Kang. But why would he…

No! The ship had smashed into rocks from the angry giant's rage. The captain, in his haste to escape prying eyes, decided to skim along the coastline to avoid rough seas and the presence of disapproving ships that patrol the waters of the African coast. Large openings tore through the body of the long boat. Those shackled had no chance to escape the water's assault. Numair could see some were a bit shaken and frightened as they were being freed. But still others were not so fortunate.

Kang holds the boy firm; he controls his entire body with his grip. It is far more intimidating than that of his father. But Numair could sense that its purpose was not to keep him out of the way. Now lifeless bodies pass the two as the captors carry them out as though they were rubbish, the young prince knew them all. Ten to fifteen bodies come their way before Kang ushers them top ward. He sits Numair at the center of the long boat and looks at him with intensity! He turns and walks a short distance and returns with… the boy's bounty! In his haste, Numair became oblivious to it and must have tossed it to the side. Kang knows who this belongs to. Numair cares not about the consequences at the moment. He comes in close to the boy and stares for a moment… then Kang places a hand on his shoulder as if to say, "It's alright."

Again, he has taken the boy by surprise with his actions. And again, Numair wonders, who is he and where does he come from? Numair admires him and is in total awe of his prowess. But that is not what's on the boy's mind at the moment. He needs to see who has fallen. He must get closer or at least have the opportunity to view all that are passed through.

The number of bodies becomes overwhelming, so he is ushered topside. He struggles, but with no success. He must account for his family. Where are they? The suspense is unbearable.

CHAPTER 3

PROPHECIES UNFOLD

A jungle cove, lit only by a huge roaring fire pit, is secluded and yet full of activity this night. Restrained against an enormous boulder is a very muscular, but older male. He has the marks from countless battles throughout his body. His age is betrayed only by the salt and pepper of his hair. He is mighty to behold, he is defiant in stature, he is imposing… he is a captive!

Three figures are gathered with the captive. A man, ominous in figure, breaks the silence with a commanding voice.

He is garishly garbed in hideous war costume. He resembles a jackal in his outfit and has dried blood throughout his body and hair.

Menacing indeed, he is Onkala. The most formidable rival chieftain from a neighboring tribe and a most vile man whose manner is very gauche. He barks his command to one of the three accompanying the captive. It is Sammiel, Numair's uncle. He has a look of satisfaction on his face.

"Your bounty awaits you. Everything that has passed will have no reward until all is finished! Your king," as he spits on the earth. "Your king has held you from what should be rightfully yours long enough! With this act, our alignment will be complete," he shouts. "Our merger will create the mighty nation needed to conquer all the lands! King Chimeratu, thank you..." as he laughs, "for building such a fine treasure. Your people, the land, and your wealth will be used to build a mighty nation!"

"Sammiel, my son," the mighty king interjects. "This thing you have done, although you think that you have accomplished your dream, this is something that was foretold ages ago! Your betrayal had to take place! Know that you have set in motion a greatness that will never die! It will evolve and grow ever stronger with each generation, void of you! Savor your victory, child! The bitterness of this betrayal shall ravage your bodies! You both will suffer terror like no one has ever seen!"

With a hardy laugh, the mighty king begins a chant. It begins as a murmur and grows in its intensity. "Hear me fathers of my fathers, the time has come for our destiny to begin. Give of the gift foretold long ago. Hear your child and bring forth the power of the chosen. Hear me fathers of my fathers, the time has come for our destiny to begin. Give of the gift foretold long ago. Hear your child and bring forth the power of the chosen." At the very height of the king's chant, the blade pierces his flesh! His mighty heart continues to beat around the blade as it pushes through him. His eyes focus forward; he continues his chant until… he smiles. The hand that inflicts the damage releases its grip. It is Sammiel. He has done this, but does not understand the cryptic message from his father!

Breathing heavily and totally entranced by his deed, he is oblivious to the disturbance behind him. At that moment the thick veiled jungle is rustling from two directions. The accomplice faces reveal the shock and fear present. They poise their bodies to the ready, weapons held firm. The stirring causes Sammiel to turn and bear witness. His bravado suddenly gives way to sheer terror! Horror and fear now take the center stage in his demeanor.

"No! This cannot be!" His eyes reveal the outcome. For from the jungle appear two giant panthers, black as a starless night!

They pause as if to allow for their presence to be fully absorbed. They slowly advance, stopping only to acknowledge one another and begin a full out charge toward the parties in their path.

Sammiel turns his attention with full outright rage, only to find his father glaring at him with a smile. At that very moment, every ounce of hatred bubbled to the surfaces from within Sammiel! It is with a mighty roar and an even more intense strike, a king is headless.

A sudden hush envelops the scene, the stars are once again gathered in this one location as in previous times. It is as though the air stands still and all manner of life is now motionless. That is all about those involved. In this case it is a party of one, Sammiel! This is his moment in the journals of time. For he now understands his role in the family. He never imagined that it would be him to set in motion the release of the gift. He was told from a young age that because of heritage, he was destined to receive the gift. But this is not to be, for it is the opposite of what he has known all of his life!

Now faced with the unrelenting truth, Sammiel does not accept his fate. In that brief moment he has decided to take control of his own destiny and alter the course of a prophecy. In that instant, Sammiel's fears give way to rage and even more hatred than ever before. He now sees the entire plan laid before him. He understands what must be done in order for him to change the fates.

Now armed with a newfound purpose, he regains his focus and sets out to take the challenges head on. He first must dispatch the impending onslaught that faces. This is the task that will allow him to proceed further.

Now focused on the two menacing figures before him, he glares into the abyss of their gaze. He does not prepare for battle. He only keeps his gaze upon the giant beasts. The panthers are motionless and only glare back at the group of men. They simultaneously view the fallen king. At the moment, they begin a slow survey of their area. Once again acknowledging one another with a glance, a brief pause, and their mission is clear!

The two panthers advance with lightning speed. Both panthers pounce simultaneously! The other men scream in horror as their spears brace for impact. But their assault is for Sammiel! As he grapples with his deed, the two panthers merge! As it descends nears its target… it fades into nothing. At that very instant, the fire roars towards the heavens.

All that can be heard is the crackle of the flames… and the pounding of terrified hearts filled with rushing blood, ignited by pure fear. It is moments before the silence is broken not by cheers, but by glances of astonishment and disbelief. Gathering their composure the triumphant party regroups. Finally words pierce the air when Sammiel orders that a pyre be built.

Having committed the unspeakable against his father, he orders one of the men to release the old man's body from its bindings against the boulder. Some men hesitantly approach and begin the process of releasing the lifeless body from its bindings. A glance among themselves speaks volumes as to the gravity of what they have just witnessed and accomplished. They continue as commanded, and the body drops to the ground in a sickening heap. It is then that Sammiel gestures toward the pyre and the body is placed there. The severed head of the once proud king is placed in his hands upon his chest. In the blink of an eye the fire is ignited. Smoke billows towards the heavens as the flames become more intense, engulfing the fallen monarch's lifeless body. The triumphant party looks into the flames as the fire ravages the remains, most stare in victory, while one looks for something more.

Confident that the body is being destroyed, the party simply gathers their belongings and leaves the thicket. No words are spoken as they disappear into the canopy of jungle night. A single glance back is all that Sammiel can bring himself to do, for he knows that he has altered his destiny forever and there can be no turning back. And then they are gone.

The African skies are abundant with stars this night; many have come to call it, "The night of the gathering." The pyre burns itself and the remains down to a pile of ashes. Embers crackle and tumble amongst the remains. The night is still, all is a hush. With nothing and no one around, there is a stirring from the pyre.

As the embers glow and the fire dies, a ghostly image appears. It surveys its surroundings, looks towards the heavens and smiles. Bringing its glance down to view the departure area of the group that has just left. Its eyes reveal nothing, just a familiar glow. It is then that the specter turns his gaze to the west. With the slightest motion it is gone!

CHAPTER 4

Captives

The rain is pelting from all angles. The huge wall of water still crashing against the longboat causes many to lose their footing. Numair is oblivious to the conditions as he is focused upon family and nothing else. Then he finds relief, for the next living person to be ushered topside lifts his hopes and causes him to react as the child he is. He breaks free of the grasp, or was allowed free, to run to her. As Numair comes closer, she looks saddened and is openly allowing tears to stream down her face… but why? He does not want to see any more is what his spirit is telling him, but his heart yearns to know… Grandmother!

It is at the very next moment that the waiting is over… his father's lifeless body is hauled topside. Time seems to crawl to an almost halt. The sight freezes the blood in Numair's veins. His eyes in disbelief, he stares at every inch of his father's body. In what seems like hours, in reality is only a few moments, Numair replays numerous interactions with was his father. Tears well up in the boys eyes and his heart is heavy. The men carrying his body move toward the side of the longboat to discard the body as they have done the rest. The boy runs to his father's lifeless body and embraces him with all of his might! His tears are lost in the downpour of rain, but the love for his father is ever apparent. He feels as though he is torn apart and totally empty. All of this is insane, their lives uprooted, destroyed, and betrayed, and for what? His father, his beloved father, wait! Where is she, where is his mother? He cannot lose her as well! Please, ancestors, do not be so cruel, he pleads! Through all of the chaos of the storm, he sees her; mother is alive, but she is also distraught. She loved her husband, and it was their bond that forged their family's strength. Numair goes to comfort her when all sound is silenced, all activity ceases motion. It is as if the air stops and the planet halts. Only he is in motion and aware of what is transpiring… what is happening. He has no time for fear, when from nothing appears two luminescent panthers. One to the right of him and the other to the left, they stand majestic and proud. With a noble and strong stride, they approach… Numair. Strangely, he is not afraid, just amazed. As they near him, he hears his father's voice.

"Numair."

It is faint at first, but it is repeated,

"Numair!"

It is the panther to the right who is speaking. Shock gives way to something familiar… the eyes! As they glow, he can sense his father's presence. He feels the warmth and love. IT IS HIS FATHER! But how can this be? Has he too died and passed through the ancestral mountains?

"Numair, do not fear, my son. It is time."

As he pauses, Numair is puzzled by this statement. Time for what, is this a crazy dream? Now the panther to the left speaks,

"You are not mad, my grandchild."

Grandchild, this cannot be!

"Grandfather?"

"Yes, little king, it is I. And you are not mad," as he bellows out his distinguishable laugh.

"It is you and father, you are not dead," replies Numair!

"We are no longer of this world, but have now ascended to the ancestral plain. We have merged with your forefathers. And the time has come for the creation and passing of the essence long ago foretold. You are the first in a very long line of true kings that will possess this power. It can only be received by a true heir."

"What power, and why me?" tearfully asks Numair. "Father, you should be the one, the one to take this on. I am merely a child! I don't want a power; I only want you two again," the saddened Numair contends.

Again that hearty laugh from his grandfather, "Numair, child, this thing that has transpired had to have taken place in order for the people and land to be protected. We will always love you and be with you. But now you must be strong and be ever vigilant. For others know of your coming of age and are plotting as we speak, of how to destroy you and your destiny. Listen carefully, long ago it was foretold that our family would have a gift bestowed upon us. The time was never revealed nor the member of the bloodline who would receive this gift. It was said to be a gift of such great power that it would change the world! For a century, the elder members of the family would be informed of the prophecy and what the details would hold. We were all told once it became clear that we were not the chosen one. Until one drunken night with a concubine, your grandfather told the tale to one of his lovers."

"How many times am I going to have to hear that it was my fault?" grandfather shouts.

He finds it amusing that two panthers are arguing.

"That was the night that all of their lives would change forever. This is where your journey began, even before you were born. But it is also the night that your enemies became aware of you and sought to destroy not only you, but the royal family as well. From that dreaded moment, you have been hunted and will continue to be hunted until you have reached your full potential. It is then that you can conquer your enemy. You will build a new kingdom that will usher in a new way of life for our people, who will also change due to your efforts. You will take on a journey unlike any before. Fear not and never falter, for we will be with you every step of the way. On your journey, you are to learn every lesson that comes to you. Some lessons will be hard to believe or bear witness to. But fear not, little king, this too must pass in order for the gift to complete its journey to you. For now, go to your mother and grandmother. They will need your strength and resolve to lend in your growth. You will have many teachers. You must see that in every encounter. Many will not know that they are instructing you. You have an excellent teacher now and your destinies will intertwine for some time. Learn everything, for as the first of your kind, you will need to be a vessel of knowledge, wisdom, patience, compassion, and strength. All of these are now magnified and have superior capabilities over your enemies. But you must remain just, for there is a failsafe for those who will seek to abuse the power and you must not succumb to the allure of dominance. All will be glorious once you conclude this journey. But you have an abundance of work ahead of you. When the time is right, you will know your full power and victory will be yours. But now your journey begins, not here, but at the edge of the motherland. You will trek a great distance; your destination, our homeland, will be different from what you remember, but it is there that you will reveal yourself to our people and the world! But Numair, this is no longer to be our home. Your task will be to gather together our people and bring them to a better world. You and the people must prosper. For the land that is destined for our new home is of great importance to many, some of which you are not aware of nor they of you. For our people to survive and prosper, you must first send out many to distant parts of the world as envoys to your kingdom. And they will bring to you vast knowledge yet unrevealed to our people. Take this knowledge and expand our culture and her people. For you are to usher in a new dawn of man!"

And with that, the panther claiming to be Numair's father winks at him and bows in reassurance.

"And tell that old woman that I love her and wait for the day that we are once again joined together in the ancestral plain. And that I hope that her cooking improves… blah," says the one panther who proclaims to be his grandfather.

"Numair, you are not hurt! Thank you, ancestors!"

What? He is again in the storm and he is hearing his grandmother. They are smothering him with affection. But, he was just… Before he can finish the thought, an oaf takes hold of his mother by her hair and attempts to drag her away! Without hesitation, Numair pounces with a primal instinct, but this time he is aware. He lands around the grizzled violator's shoulders. And with little effort, he tosses the oaf to the side as though he were a broken jug. This incites another filthy warthog to attack; he too is dispatched with no effort. Numair drops with such flexibility to his side and gives way to a most powerful kick! That kick sends the strange and filthy man down into the hold with the oncoming waters. He springs back to an upright position and stands at the ready.

But no others follow suit. His senses relax and he can see astonishment on everyone's faces. Even Numair's family is in awe of what has just happened. He too has to admit, the rush took him by surprise, but the energy that he felt leaves him in amazement. Then he realizes that he may have allowed too much to be realized too soon. So he must act quickly! He runs to his mother and grandmother, as he nears them, stumbles and falls. He bruises his knee enough to draw blood and begins to cry. He needs their attention and motherly love now. As they embrace him and tend to his wound, the clever prince surveys his audience and everyone is carrying on with their business, but he can sense the lingering suspicion.

"Land HO!"

Rich black soil, fertile and abundant with life, covers the mountain basin. Beautiful flowers sway back and forth with the flow of the winds. Sunrays have little obstruction as few clouds are scattered across the beautiful blue skies. Small creatures scurry along the thick patches of grass. Birds of many varieties feast on the multitude of animals and insects that flourish in this seemingly untouched-by-man terrain. But the land has been traveled.

High above the trees, a bird of prey eyes the land below. It spies a snake-like formation but gives the impression of familiarity. For it has seen this particular animal many times and knows that it is not what it seems. Although it is many times larger than anything that the spying eyes have seen and longer than any animal that it has seen, it has many legs. It always moves so carefully and focused. Each step that it takes lands perfectly in the same position as the foot before it, thereby doing little to disturb the surrounding landscape. The band of unknowns travels at a modest pace, yet ever so watchful. From the front of the caravan, a voice can be heard to say, "Come now. Our destination is just a little further ahead."

The voice is strong yet pleasant to the senses. The travelers are all masked and clothed from head to toe. Light weapons and shiny shields accompany each member of the band of travelers. Attached to a few backs are large sacks fashioned from animal hides, as well as provisions and water. It is the glimmer of the sunrays bouncing from the metal shields and weapons that catches the bird of prey's attention. But if it notices their presence, what or who else has as well? Small herds of migrating wildlife pause to take notice of the strange sight. But the attention of the animals shifts to the rear of the party. A sight not unnoticed by the lead person of the caravan.

"Hurry! Keep moving, we're nearly there," commands the voice.

But there is a sense of urgency in the tone. Taking leave of the formation to the side and positioning upon a small ridge along their path to look back. Glancing up at their leader, only a shape can be seen due to the glaring sunlight behind it. But it is undeniably the shape of a woman. A statuesque and curvaceous figure is all that can be discerned, yet remarkably unforgettable. The woman peers off into the distance to spy a small band of assailants making a hasty charge towards her party.

"RUN!" she shouts to her band of travelers.

And run they do. Swift and fleet of foot, never breaking formation, the group pushes forward and rounds the basin's bend. The woman chooses to fall to the rear of the formation.

"They are not to escape!" shouts the raider's commander.

He and his horde of marauders are members of Lord Sammiel's ever-expanding empire. An empire that either absorbs a people or, more often than not, enslaves them. Today they have their sights set on this group in particular. They know not why they must capture their prey, they only know that it is wise to heed any commands of Lord Sammiel. The raider commander roars, "Faster, you jackals! We shall please our lord and master with this prize."

And faster they are. The quickened pace shortens the distance between the two parties. Both parties race along the mountain basin. The unknown people round the basin and the female leader has now regained the point position. And within a few steps, a strange dense cloud of fog engulfs the basin from seemingly thin air. As the final member of the woman's party enters the fog, the raiders round the basin and are halted in awe. For the view of the raiders, the other side of the mountain basin is a haven for a large troop of baboons. There is no fog nor are their intended targets. It is as if the unknown people were simply swallowed up by the earth. Yet there is no time for the raiders to ponder the situation, for the troop of baboons has now taken on an aggressive posture. Several large male baboons bare their lengthy and razor-sharp fangs in warning. The raider commander keeps his wits about himself and orders his men to slowly retreat.

The raider's leader is no different from most of the inhabitants of these lands. Fraught with superstitions and the unexplainable, although he cannot explain what they just bore witness to, he does understand that there can be no excuse for failure. So he commands his men to never speak of this incident or suffer the wrath of Lord Sammiel. A fact that is unanimously agreed upon. The raiders trek back to the open plains and to their scout and plunder mission.

CHAPTER 5

BIRTH OF CHAOS

To understand how this proud family came into prominence, one would have to go back to the beginning. The moments that spark the creation of this royal family, this tormented family.

"Victory is ours!" Cheers resound throughout. Tonight is glorious, for today's defeat of the last of the terror of the land ends many years of warring and bloodshed. Tonight is more than just a victory celebration. It is the ushering in of a new beginning for all of the tribes. A new breath of life throughout the land has culminated today. And the spearhead of today's events is the newly crowned king!

Today begins the reign of King Chimeratu! He is regal on the platform and a sight to behold! He towers over ordinary men. His presence commands attention and his voice is like that of thunder. Yet this giant of a man is also a statesman, for tonight he has gathered all of the tormented and downtrodden tribes from all corners of the land to begin talks of peace. The celebration and peace talks are to carry on for a week.

The king makes an announcement to the masses. An event of this magnitude has never occurred except on the battlefield. Once mortal enemies, multiple tribes are joined together for one single purpose, the end of eternal bloodletting is the bond that brings them together and all the people are of one mind. Men, women, children, young and old alike, all as one! It is a beautiful sight. "People of the Motherland, today marks our new lives," he begins. "We have suffered at the hands of the hordes of evil men for far too long."

"Men who promised everything, took all, and delivered horror and suffering! This time, together, we shall forge an alliance that will truly serve the people. We shall merge together as one unified people of this great land. We will set the standards to serve all and lead us to prosperity together!" Cheers welcome his mighty words as he descends the platform. His wife, ever beside him, she is his beloved and with child. At any moment, a new life may come. His concern for her is his first priority. But she is now Queen Akilah, a beauty that many men fought over. Her beauty is known throughout the lands. Her physical beauty paled in comparison to her compassion and graceful nature. But the one element that made her ever more the fairest of the lands is her fiery nature. On several occasions, her village was attacked, and it was said that she fought as fierce as the most renowned warrior. But one man was chosen, the now savior of the people of the Motherland, mighty Chimeratu.

It is said that while the queen enjoyed the attention of the suitors, she always looked beyond them for someone. It was not until the night of the battle of the western land that she saw him. Chimeratu was the western lands' mightiest warrior. He and his tribes came to Akilah's village to seek aid in the fight. He marched his people proudly into the heart of the village. It is a marvel to witness the precision that they exercised. There has never been such a military unit witnessed before. It was always a mass of bodies stabbing at anyone not recognized. Chimeratu used units of fighters to overcome their enemies. Their opponents never could compensate for the lack of structure and thus succumb to the well-organized fighting units of the western lands. From his father, Chimeratu studied the ways of men and the cause and effect of different actions. He studied the lands before a battle, learned of pitfalls and their locations. Avoided obstacles before they became an issue, he was a warrior statesman.

His reputation preceded him as Akilah's father, Chief Dakarai, has the counsel in session to hear the powerful warrior's proposal. As is her village custom, the counsel sessions are held in the center of the village. The ideas being that all have a say in the direction of the village. The counsel weighs the input and votes on the final outcome for all to view. It is a noble idea and the people are content that nothing is done without their knowledge. But it is here that the glance beyond the many suitors finds what her heart and body have been searching for. At that very moment, a warrior whose thoughts have always been focused on ending tyranny and oppression by any means necessary. Suddenly becomes as gentle as a quiet stream. All around him seems to disappear and the only being within his view is Akilah! Their gazes are known by all. It is no secret from that moment on that they are star-crossed lovers to be.

After counsel the night before, a magnificent battle ensues that leaves the mighty Chimeratu once again victorious. Like the other villages that have joined forces with Chimeratu, he keeps his word and the village is now free to choose its own destiny. He imposes no claim to the people of the village, but instead pledges to honor their kinship as part of the agreement to aid in the fight against their common enemies. To show honor and gratitude, Chief Dakarai asks the great warrior what can be offered to stand as a reward. With a curious look on Chimeratu's face, an answer is rendered. "I only seek to be joined as a member of this great tribe!" Cheers are shouted as the entire village welcomes such an addition into their folds; that is all but Akilah. She quietly saunters up to her father's side and positions herself. She looks into her father's eyes and he knows that something powerful is about to take place.

"Mighty Chimeratu, your request is quite humble, flattering, and welcomed by all," she says. "A welcome addition indeed, but there is something that everyone has overlooked!" The cheers come to an abrupt halt! Chief Dakarai calmly asks his daughter to please explain herself. "Surely father, you and all gathered have not forgotten that in order to be one with this tribe, strangers of a different tribe, man or woman, must take a mate of the village?"

"Akilah is right, mighty Chimeratu," said Chief Dakarai. "It is our custom from long ago to allow only the finest stock of men and women may be welcomed into the village to be assured of a strong foundation to be passed down through the generations. We have always…" before he could finish his statement, Akilah again takes center. "But mighty Chimeratu, I will save you the trouble of the ritualistic selection process and offer myself to you as your wife," as she pounds her chest in a commanding manner. She gracefully turns and again takes her astonished father's side.

It is truly amusing to see such a sight to Chimeratu, but he doesn't hesitate for a moment to render his answer. A resounding "Yes" could be heard across the land! The couple is united within a short time, for Chimeratu's family made the journey to witness their son's blessed day. It is at this time that a revelation comes about. Chimeratu's parents are the king and queen of the western tribes!

King Chima and Queen Chika are known for their fair and impartial monarchy. The queen is renowned for her beauty and grace and for her strength of character. King Chima is known throughout the land for his fierce fighting and his diplomacy throughout the tribes. Strange that no one ever knew that Chimeratu was their son, odd indeed.

The union proceeded, and the couple began a legacy of unity, justice, and fair and impartial reign. There are many tales of how the queen fought beside the king in many battles. The history of this power couple is legendary. Their love is exhibited by their doting on their son, prince Chimeratu. Tonight ignites the cornerstone for unifying several tribes and creating a single powerful nation. A nation far more advanced than any tribe in the land.

There is much drinking and laughter. But all are not rejoicing as the others. No, eyes of a few have another agenda and possible celebration to look forward to. Watchful eyes remain trained on the king, for they have a purpose, a purpose that lay in wait for the most opportune time. As the king greets his people and rejoices with them, he is offered a drink, a drink that was specially made in secret. It has ingredients of a special nature and a defined purpose.

A grizzled hand carefully mixes the concoction to ensure that the desired effect is achieved. "Your majesty, please accept this cool drink as a token of our gesture of thanks for all that you have done for the people and the land."

"Thank you," says the king as he lifts his drink high and gives cheer to all. As the king returns his gaze to his presenter, she is gone. A small, unassuming figure blends into the crowd and vanishes among the masses. Triumphant in her cause, a woman greets another woman. "He has the potion and now it is up to you, my daughter."

"You must not leave his presence, for the mixture will take effect very quickly. And at the moment of its full strength, you must act."

"Yes mother. Are you sure that this will work?"

"Yes, this is without fail. It is you that must have the strength to fulfill your task if you are to ever reap that which you seek!"

"I can do it, mother! It is not fair that Akilah should be the only one to bear children for the king. It is not fair that only her children be assured of a future. No mother, I have the strength to fulfill my task and a purpose! I long for the day when my children will play and run beside her children and she can do nothing."

Joy of this magnitude has been absent far too long and all the people are eager to welcome the glad times. Two days into the celebration and the joy of the people is just as intense. The king stumbles to the couple's quarters and drunkenly attempts to express his desires. His groping and pawing annoy the queen so that she shouts for him to find pleasure elsewhere!

The tribal beer robs the king of his normally gentle passionate touch or his warm tender touch. From the beginning, the king has rebuffed the advances of a concubine and only had desires for his wife. A tradition shared by many kings would be to have his wife and hordes of waiting concubines at his beck and call. But not King Chimeratu! He only loved his queen and everyone knew it. Many admired him for this, yet others let their jealousy cloud the truth.

One person did feel as though the king was not being fair to others. She was Manyara, a concubine. For a concubine with a child from royalty is assured a status elevation for herself and the child, this was her desire. Throughout the celebration, she has been within reach of the royal couple, which is not uncommon. But a plan was set in motion the moment the celebration began. Manyara knew that all she had to do was to wait for the perfect moment.

"Go and sleep with the animals since you choose to behave as one," the queen shouts. "I will not have you clawing and scratching at me as though I were a carcass shared by jackals."

Without a word, although drunk, the king left the comfort of his quarters and his wife. He headed out into a clearing near the hut and slumped under a tree in the soft grass. With the cover of the night sky as his blanket, the king fell into a deep sleep. His dreams carried him back to the previous battle and the horror of the bloodshed. He tossed and turned, and his dreams turned more pleasant. He dreamt of his homecoming, of his beautiful wife waiting for him with open arms. Of her succulent body pressed next to his. He dreamt of heated pleasures, of the lovemaking and what seemed a lifetime of carnal desires shared between the two. The realism of the dream made the king sweat with passion, but the dream carried on! In the throes of passion, at one point, the queen dismounted the king from behind her and forced him onto his back. He could see darkness where there was normally a glint of joy in her eyes. He imagined that she was just as absorbed with lust for him as any man desires from the one he loves. So he gave in and allowed the lustful queen her joy. She was most aggressive in her pelvic thrusts! The king began to feel strange, as the queen, although a powerful lover, had never has shown this type of lust before. It was as if she was possessed! She was grunting and panting and scratching. She was rapid in her movements and when the king attempted to embrace her to share the moments, she would force him back to the bedding. His mind raced in ecstasy as his wife lusted for him. He just decided to enjoy the moments of pleasure and throw his head back. But the dream was turned darker! For in his dream, the trees surrounding him became a blazing inferno. He was trapped, with no way out. He struggled to gain control of his wife and make her aware of what was happening, but she never stopped. As the flames grew more intense, he could see a figure forming. He was in a struggle and was helpless. He watched as the figure became more apparent and familiar. His heart beat so powerfully that he thought it would burst from his chest. The figure was alive and moving! It gazed momentarily at the couple and then began its charge. It was a flaming panther headed straight for the lustful couple.

At the moment of the panther's leap, the king summoned all of his might to take hold of his wife, who still has not stopped her gyrations, and as he finally truly looked at her, she changed. At that very moment, the king was awake and realized that he was making love to Manyara!

Horrified, the king tossed the woman to the side and quickly pounced to his feet. Before the king could speak, a figure flashes before him and is now straddled the woman. It is Queen Akilah! "How dare you, filthy waif!"

With a mighty blow, the pregnant queen has struck the woman squarely in the face with such force that her head bounces from the grass and her nose immediately begins to bleed. At that moment King Chimeratu so outraged, draws his blade and advances towards to the down-trodden woman! But before he could, Manyara spoke. "Hold fast mighty King Chimeratu. I did not come here to upset you. I only wanted to lay with you mighty king. I am yours to do with as you please.

Please do not end my life. Forgive me for the manner in which I choose to give myself to you, Lord Chimeratu. Your highness I meant no disrespect to you. I am a concubine and it is my life's duty to give myself to the royal family. I was only acting upon that which I've trained for all of my life. Please spare me," as she sobbed tears incessantly.

Queen Akilah softened the angered king with a cooler head after listening to the woman's plight.

"My love, listen to me, a dream came to me. And in that dream, it was revealed that this moment must take place in accordance to the prophecy. Spare this wench, and we will move beyond this night. Although I know where your heart is, this indiscretion was set in motion long ago, and the course of events could not be altered." His blood boiling, Chimeratu was almost inconsolable! It wasn't until his force almost knocked his pregnant wife to the ground as he attempted to end the life of this woman. It wasn't until he heard the startled sound from his wife did he regain his senses.

"Akilah!" As he caught the queen before she fell. "I'm sorry, my love. I had no intentions of lying with this woman. I have longed for no one but you. Please believe me; I thought that she was you. It seemed so real, are you injured?"

"There is no need, my king. I am fine, but it is obvious that something was done to you this night. I have seen this reaction before. Although I do not wish for you to harm this woman, I do sense that she did not act alone. Tell me Jackal bitch, who are you in league with? Deny or lie to me and I will allow the king's guard to have their way with you and then pass you down to the captives before taking your head!"

Faced with the possibility of death, Manyara surveys her surroundings and circumstances. She feels the cage of doom ever closing in on her and cannot think clearly. This was not how it was to be. It was to be simple and precise. But her eyes betray her, as she looks beyond the gathered angry mob that has encircled her.

It is Akilah that spots the betrayal of her glance! As such, Akilah turns to see what has caught Manyara's attention. Off in the distance, she sees what or who is the object of Manyara's gaze!

"Seize her!"

And with that, the captain of the guard takes hold of Manyara's arm and tosses her down on her knees! With a mighty thrust of his spear, he plunged downward toward the back of Manyara's neck.

"STOP!"

Akilah's voice resounds throughout the night just at that very moment. With the precision of a Cobra's strike, the captain's strike is halted, but with a noticeable look of disdain for the command as well. With a piercing glance, he forcefully pulls Manyara to her feet.

"Back to the village," orders the Queen. Help the king, someone, and be careful," she commands.

She is determined in her instructions and will not be swayed.

The trek is short-lived as the group arrives back in the village center. The king is assisted to his royal sitting position. Manyara is positioned before the king and queen for further questioning. But before the proceedings began, Queen Akilah commands that Manyara be bound between to two totems, spread by all four limbs.

Tears cannot be stopped. Manyara is beside herself and cannot control her emotions or faith!

"Please, please!" she cries. But her pleas are lost to the heavens.

"Everyone come forward and witness one who has soiled your king and queen. One who has taken only her own greed and desires into accounting and, damned the sanctity of the kingdom. But she has not acted alone. And this day, she will either die or reveal her accomplice!"

"Now demon spawns, bring light upon your accomplice" shouts the queen! Her fury is clearly present and unforgiving.

But Manyara is unwavering and brings about her torture for all to witness. Her garments are ripped from the back and what comes about next, although worthy, is horrific.

Intertwined small vines tear flesh from Manyara's back! With each strike, there is a ghastly opening of white underlying flesh revealed! With each strike, Manyara screams out in agony! With each strike, the same question is asked!

"Who aided in this deed?"

There is still defiance from Manyara, who continues to protect her accomplice, her mother. Manyara's mother is among the people and she holds back her terror for her daughter's pain and suffering, yet she says nothing or gives any indication that they even know one another save for living in the same village.

That is until the queen's rage takes over her usually reasonable and presence of mind in her judgment. For the queen had had enough! For it is the queen that puts an end to the lashes. As she does so, she takes a spear from one of the guards.

With purpose, she approaches the restrained and sobering Manyara. There is hatred in her eyes, for she is acting not as a queen but a woman who is stating that her vengeance of betrayal. The crowd of the people of the new alliance watches as Akilah places the blade of the spear into the flames of the now blazing fire pit.

The onlookers all watch in approval, all but one. Manyara's mother's restraint is stretched to the limit. She is now visibly unnerved. Her face is now showing signs of worry, the worry and concern of a mother becomes ever more apparent.

Akilah approaches the beaten concubine with the searing hot blade and again asks the question.

"Who is your accomplice?"

Manyara, beaten, bloody and in total fear, can no longer stand the punishment and begins to plead for a moment.

"Please, my Queen. I will tell you, please stop!"

Not wanting her daughter to suffer any longer, the old woman breaks from the crowd. She knows that this will cease her daughter's suffering and bring all attention to her. But she runs out of the crowd, anyway! Unseen to all, a stirring is taking place within the king. His foggy haze is lifting and his mind is becoming clear, yet he is still unable to gather his thoughts for now.

Akilah's keen senses have been on high alert the entire time. This is what she has been waiting for. For she knew that Manyara's public display would trigger a reaction from her accomplice if they were still present! With a satisfied gleam in the eye, Akilah places the white hot blade to Manyara's face! Searing the flesh as a Manyara screams out in agony. And with the skill of a seasoned warrior, Akilah launches the same spear into the distance with a powerful thrust!

The spear finds its target! The old woman is halted in her place. She has a look of disbelief as she gazes down at her torso. She is impaled through and through. As life leaves her body, she shouts out to her daughter.

"I have done it, my child!"

And then she is dead.

"Let this end now!" shouts a familiar commanding voice. It is King Chimeratu! He has regained his senses and is now taking control of the situation.

"This will end now," commands the king! "You have done enough to this wretched woman and her kin. Release her and tend to her wounds," orders the king. He stands upright and assured. He has fully regained his senses and also his people. Manyara heard this and knew it to be true. "From this day forward, you shall labor as the slave to the animal herder. You will be at the mercy of his every whim. And if this is not to your pleasure, you will forfeit your life! Now go, leave my sight!"

And with that she is helped away to be tended to. Akilah is beside herself with rage, but does not offer resistance to her king. But instead, she goes to his side and embraces him.

"My love, are you alright?" She asks.

Yes, my darling, all is well now," states the mighty king. "We must not harm this woman any further. What she has done is despicable, yes, but your actions do not reflect who you are! Remember that we are not the animals that we have fought so hard to rid the land of! You are my queen and the mother of not only our child, but of this new nation."

So with that, Manyara's life is spared. The days blur and life is restored. But not long from that day, it becomes clear that Manyara succeeded in her plot to conceive. She is with child. So again, her life takes a turn, but this time it is with good fortune. She is placed in the new construction of the new royal palace. She is commissioned as the keeper of the servants of the royal family after she gives birth; but it is short-lived.

She is stripped of motherhood by the appointed counsel for her punishment for the previous crimes. The child is to be condemned to death by decree. But Chimeratu cannot let this be, so he intervenes with the reluctant support of Akilah. It is ordered that the child will be raised as a prince of the kingdom of King Chimeratu, an act that will have consequences in the future.

CHAPTER 6

FORGING THE LEGEND

They hear the cry from one of the men up high. Numair can see off in the distance the silhouette of the shoreline. He is amazed at the clarity of his eyesight. He should be terrified of what is happening to him, but he is not. He must not reveal his transformation, so he is just the fearful child who is craving his mother's arms and love.

The skies are a wall of darkness. Nothing can be seen, but only heard. Huge mountains of water batter anything on the giant river. The strange men scurry about, tying off broken and battered pieces of the long riverboat. The wood ground atop the long riverboat is very slippery. People are falling with every other step, and some are injured as they are slammed against the sides of the longboat. The fat captain is screaming with the might of a mighty lion. The men are scampering everywhere, attempting to stay ahead of the great storm. Every now and again, one of them vanishes from the side. The giant hands of the black water grab them and take them from sight.

Numair must protect his family and friends. His senses urge him to take shelter below. He takes his mother and grandmother by the hand and instructs them to do the same with the people of the village. They form a link and head down below. They make their way to the cooking area. Numair feels it is safe for all to huddle here, and there is food. No one will be mindful of this area for now. They take refuge here. Whatever fear was present among the people seems to subside. There is a quiet whispering among them. But Numair is on guard, keeping a vigilant eye open for any sign of danger.

Young Numair is oblivious to the activity in the cooking area with the people. It is not until his shoulder is gently touched by his mother. He gives her his attention and sees that the queen grandmother is there beside her. She has this strange, pleased look on her face. He says nothing, yet she does not change her expression. He looks to his mother, and she too looks strangely into his eyes. He feels awkward and must ask, "What is wrong?" His question is only answered by the same strange grin from everyone present. He can only continue his focus and keep a vigil on their current predicament. Numair cannot afford a moment's rest. He must keep his people safe from harm's way until they can find sanctuary from this mighty giant of a river.

How long they remained in the cramped quarters of their refuge, they do not know. But Numair's family and companions are well-fed and sound asleep when the sudden scuttling and cheering began. A group rushes past their location, and from their voices, Numair can tell they are jubilant about something. Numair has a choice to make: does he stay and continue to wonder what is happening, or does he take his leave and find out for himself? Numair leaves.

As Numair emerges from below, he can see the strangers embracing one another. Smiles and cheers resound throughout the ship. He notices the direction that they are concentrating their gazes. He looks off into the darkness, and there he sees it. It is not land that they cheer for, but instead, in the distance, Numair can see the impossible! He shares the strangers' joy, for out of the darkness appears another longboat but different.

He later learned that it was a warship of the British Navy. It had beautiful, crisp white sails and three masts that stood tall and regal. But at this time, all he sees is a beautiful, ornate longboat! The tall trees that carry the wind catchers are mighty. The wind catchers are unlike the tattered and grey fabrics of this longboat. They are beautifully white as the sky puffs. And the people are so different. They are clean and beautiful in their appearances. Their clothes are full of color and are vibrant, so different from the filthy men on this longboat.

This longboat glides across the giant river, and although far off, it moves effortlessly across the water. The young prince sees giant spines piercing its sides. But it is not like something wounded the longboat;

rather, the longboat has the things as round metal spikes from the inside. They have what appear to be wooden eyelids over each spike—strange indeed. He sees many people moving about, but unlike the dirty men of this longboat, these people seem to move with purpose and structure. There are men with very decorative headwear and some with simple headwear with what appear to be tails! Humorous looking as it is, they are well-organized and obedient to the obvious captain of their longboat. Numair believes this is obvious, as the captain has the most ornate headwear and body covering. Each time he speaks, everyone moves and renders a strange sign of obedience to him with their hands. He stands at the high end of the longboat and has a few men near him, but it is clear that he is the high command. There is something else onboard this strange longboat—there are women! There are two elder and three younger women. They stand on the high end with the master of the longboat. Their appearances are of large melons with legs. They too have headwear, and they are fully clothed from their necks to the ground. He cannot help but wonder how it is possible for them to move. The child of the jungle cannot see that they have feet. Their bottoms are covered in fine cloth, but there is so much of the cloth!

Numair pauses for a moment to notice that he is seeing all of this as though he were standing right next to these people. Yet the new longboat is a great distance from our location. It has become apparent to him that this has not been a dream! He has some type of ability, and it is growing ever more powerful. Numair had "the gift"; he was "the chosen one"! Numair realized that none of this had been a dream. His ancestors had appeared to him, and what his father and grandfather have said to him is true.

The realization of this is bittersweet. In one night, he has lost his father and has been given the fabled "ancestral gift." This moment has his destiny to reveal itself with the purest clarity. Numair is the true king and now has the responsibility of reuniting his people and their lands. But more importantly, he must save the people and salvage their future from the dark pits they find themselves in. For most, this would seem as though the weight of the universe were upon their shoulders. But not King Numair, for in those sorrowful moments, a transformation occurred. Numair's entire demeanor changed. Internally and physically, the boy king's manifestation was apparent to his people. His mother cried, not at their turmoil, but rather in the sheer elation of her son's blessing! That is only curbed by the all-too-real realization that her son is now the ruler of a damaged kingdom and its people. She cannot overlook the fact that now more than ever, her son's new station in life has given rise to him shining like a beacon. His rebirth now will call upon all who oppose their nation. Most importantly, Sammiel will become aware of his existence!

The dawn is coming, and the rains are leaving with the night. With each passing moment, the new longboat is closer. Their current longboat is taking on water much faster now. But it has been confined to the one area of the longboat that took the life of Numair's father and many others. Focus, focus! He must keep his mind on the task at hand. Get the family to safety. Rushing below, he reaches the cooking area. The area is crowed along the passage. As Numair enters, he again notices that his people are paying homage to him. All eyes are upon him, viewing him with reverence. Muffled voices can be heard. Bodies part, giving way to Numair as a clear sign of respect and awe. He decides not to let them all know that he has become aware of his transformation, that must be addressed another time. For now, he must ensure that they all make it to the top and be seen by the new longboat.

And seen they are! While the horrific loss of Numair's father and country brethren and sisters was taking place. Through the flashes of lightning, in the distance, an outline of what could only deemed as another ship! The death of his father and his kinsmen is a mix of emotions for everyone. Everyone except Numair. He has come to understand his intestinal fortitude. He is maturing far beyond his years. Not only physically and emotionally, but mentally as well. Time seems to slow down. That is to him. But in reality, it is but a few moments. During this time, pandemonium is running amuck. The strange men scramble about and voices cannot be distinguished from the roar of the storm. The captain shouted and others repeated his words as they all scrambled to keep the longboat afloat and make their presence known. This situation needed no interpretation, all understood the gravity of the moment. At that moment, Numair gave instructions to his people to assist with preserving the ship and to maintain the fires now burning in the designated fire stations. They were normally used as simple lighting for visibility during the night watch. Initially, the captures ran about, slipping and falling over the wet deck or into each other. But the Numair ordered the people to assist, order came at once. Initially, the people's assistance was met with apprehension and suspension. At the start of these helpful gestures, the captain pushed through the bewildered group of men and headed towards the now free roaming cargo. Despite knowing that they were now free due the circumstances of the night and not wanting to lose the precious cargo. He was about to speak when he was left speechless by what he witnessed. The cargo somehow not only assisted the captures, but knew how to assist them. As the pelting rain continues to assault the men and women. The collective efforts bring the long boat about to align directly towards the oncoming vessel. In an instant, the captain disregards his ego and begins to work together with all to salvage this doomed ship for as long as possible. And then it happens. The distant vessel lights its fires in recognition of the sinking craft. And immediately increases its speed to come forth without haste, the beautiful longboat is alongside their current sinking longboat, and people are being transported to safety as quickly as possible. Numair and his people are stunned to witness the pale rescuers separate the filthy pale men from the rest.

It is another lesson that Numair will not forget. He does not embrace moments such as this, but rather stores them in his mind to build upon in his journey through life.

Days have passed, and Numair and his people have yet another challenge to face. They survived the imprisonment of the longboat and the giant river, only to face a new form of captivity. The people are now housed in a dark and dank large barred room beneath a very large structure. There is little comfort from the cold, damp stone floor that now serves as their sleeping quarters. The heavy bars show their signs of age and weather-worn wear. Heavy rust and other materials cake the floor-to-ceiling cages and windows. The air is stale and foul, yet it is a vast improvement from the death- and feces-filled cramped quarters of the disgusting longboat that held them stacked upon one another for more than a month. Nor do they have to endure the shackles that bound them to the belly of the longboat. The glimmer of sunlight is that they are no longer stacked upon one another as they were previously upon the disastrous ship that stole them to begin with, or shackled and unable to move. There is another difference between these quarters and the ship: all of the women and children, except for a few men, are in this room. The remaining men are housed out in the elements in very large cages. There are no walls to pretend to shield them from the elements. There is filth and mud as their beds. But they are alive. For the first time in some time, all of the people are able to view the sun and the heavens. A thing that is often taken for granted by many is viewed as a gift from the ancient ones. Numair and his people truly give thanks for this, and for tonight, the rest is peaceful.

The dawn brings more of the strangely clothed pale people. It is a humiliating time as they flock to see the dark savages as if they were on display. Despicable and inhuman, yet the gallery of gawkers increases with every moment. Some stare and point, while others mock and throw food, mud clumps, and rocks at the defenseless souls locked in the cages. The morning sun shines bright, and there is a small cloud cover. Perfect for the pale families to make a day of another being's suffrage. The sleepy coastal port is still in its infant stages of growth. Daily routines are mundane and physically taxing. There is little entertainment to speak of. A small faction of Christians, varying in small sects, goes about the business of spreading their gospel and establishing a foothold in this little fishing village. The village is unlike other coastal shanty towns in that it has several solid structures. There is a livery stable that houses several animals besides horses. A stockyard for taking and auctioning the imported livestock from different lands. A dry goods store services the people of the town and doubles as the town's lending establishment. There are two import and export houses. They stock and store goods for trade. They are owned by two different individuals. There are several churches of different denominations. The most affluent being the Catholic Church. The next in terms of influence is a Baptist church that is looked down upon by the Catholics, yet it has some very influential and powerful members among its numbers. There are also two room and board establishments that house weary seafarers while in port. For travelers and some of the residents, there are several taverns to choose from. Each tavern has an assorted mix of spirits, games of chance, and a bevy of women who seek to comfort any lonely traveler… for a fee. There is a theater that offers a bit of culture for the residents, but its patronage is small. After all, this is a shipping port with very few aristocrats frequenting. The popular port's location and successful trade routes allow for all businesses to thrive. And there is the current location. It is the town's civic center. It is the town hall, courthouse, and stockade.

CHAPTER 7

EVIL'S SPAWN

A lone drop from a single blade of grass is the last thing that the eyes of a dying man see. Time has stopped as he watches the single drop release from the grass stalk and makes its descent downward to rejoin with the land. He is not aware of anything around him. He sheds a single tear… And as the blood makes contacts with the earth, the life spark fades from the dying man.

Screams of terrified villagers fill the air! "Burn everything!" a voice shouts. A woman is running for her life through all of the carnage when she is speared from behind from the very carnage that she is desperately trying to escape. Her body falls forward into a burning structure set ablaze due to the course of the raid earlier. She screams in agony as the flames engulf her body and life. Hers is not the only voice to resound the scene that is taking place. Flames dance throughout the village. Bodies are strewn about signifying the horrors that is taking place.

"Sammiel we have taken the village," a death covered warrior pronounces. "Shall we begin the gathering of survivors?"

"No! This village will be a testament to our power. I want nothing or no one left alive. KILL THEM ALL!" Sammiel peers at the death around him as flames paint images across his face. His eyes are black and void of emotions. A group of captive villagers scream their last breaths of life as spears and knives plunge into flesh. Throats are cuts as blood splashes to the earth. "Run child, run!" a lone woman shouts as a small girl hears her pleas and runs for her life. A brute of a man appears from around a structure and with a single thrust… the girl is impaled on a very large knife.

As the air is blanketed with the foul smell of burning flesh and blood, the lone master slayer surveys his conquest. The stars catch a glimpse of what lies behind the dark eyes. Tonight and the nights before this are only a small testament of what is to come…

The murderous army makes its way back to its stronghold. Sammiel marches past the masses and heads directly to his quarters. It is huge and ornate. He lavishes in his conquests from his pillaging. As he enters, guards immediately assume their post outside of his area. Inside Sammiel pauses… his mind wanders. He is interrupted by the handmaiden that he chose. She brings his drink, a thick gruel of beer. He gulps down the thick brew swiftly and demands another. It is obvious that he has something on his mind. It is not long before the woman returns with the beer. Once Sammiel takes the drink, she turns to leave bowing, but she is halted by his grasp! She dare not struggle nor protest. As he gulps down the beer, he draws her near. His arm encircles her across her neck and chest. As he finishes the last of the drink, he tosses the container to the other side of the quarters. He spins the woman around and takes the serving tray from her and tosses it as well. At the same time he tosses the woman to his bed. She knows what is about to happen and braces herself with a trance-like state. She does not love him and knows that he does not love her. He feels entitled to whatever he wants and will be merciless to any opposition to his belief.

Sammiel is void of emotions. He is acting on animal lust. He cares not for the woman's desires, only his primal needs. He throws the woman onto her belly and tears her clothing from her body. He loosens his loin cloth with his freehand and viciously enters the woman with no regard for her. He pounds her with bad intentions and holds her by her hair and hips. The woman turns as a reaction to the powerful thrusts and quickly has her head pushed down into the bedding. She raises her head to breathe and again takes her mind to a distant memory. She must endure for her life's sake. The pounding and thrusting continue, but Sammiel is not satisfied. As he violates the woman, he demands, "Do I not please you?" Without hesitation the woman replies, "No man has ever pleased me so, my lord!" with each word briefly paused to accommodate for the lustful thrusts of Sammiel. This temporarily appeases Sammiel, but does not convince him. He becomes more aggressive in his brutal assault on the woman and pulls out from her body. As she gathers herself and begins to turn to stand, Sammiel takes her by her hair and grips her face so hard that it forces her to open her mouth in pain. At that moment he places himself in her mouth and again begins to defile her orally. She does nothing but pray that he will be content and end this brutality soon. And just as abrupt as it began, Sammiel tenses his body, makes a powerful noise and releases his foul seed. It is over! The woman makes no qualms about what just occurred, she simply dresses, gathers her serving tray and leaves.

Sammiel, satisfied with the deed, falls down on the bedding and pants with relief physically appeased. But his mind does not rest. As he continues to breathe heavily, he has a moment of reflection. He remembers taking his father's life and the path he took to obtain a prize. But why has he not received the gift? His brothers are no more, dead or near death and his father and mother are of no concern any longer. The people are his to command, yet he remains unrewarded.

Did I overlook something? he ponders. There is no one who can oppose me, so why, am I not embodied with the gift! Why, why, why?

Could it be? It cannot be that simple can it? Of course, I must be singular in my reign. I did not think that I would have to rid myself of this pestilence so soon. I understand now that I have one last task to complete my ascendance to the throne, it is time. With piercing eyes, Sammiel envisions his treacherous action.

At that very moment the entrance to Sammiel's chamber burst inward. A hearty laugh and bold smile engulf Onkala's face. "We have done it!" No one can oppose our reign now. We have the entire region bowing to our feet, boldly pronounces Onkala. I knew we were destined to join forces and rule these lands..... hahahaha, says Onkala as he flops himself onto the seating inside of Sammiel's quarters. His words fall upon deaf ears. Sammiel's mind is far away. He is oblivious to his surroundings. "Tonight we begin our celebration....YES!" A celebration is a fitting manner to begin the triumphant union of power....hahahaha, cackles Onkala. With a pounce to his feet, Onkala bursts through the opening of Sammiel's quarters! "Tonight we celebrate our victory and dawn of the new order of the land! Shouts Onkala to the tribesmen and villagers." A murmur is uttered by Sammiel, "a celebration... yes," as if preoccupied by other matters. But then his focus returns and he joins Onkala in his jubilation. "A feast for your returning conquers and rulers of the land!" shouts Sammiel. But his gaze is not to the people, but upon Onkala who does not notice.

"I must rest before tonight's festivities," announces Sammiel. "Of course," says Onkala. "I too must take my leave in or to prepare for the festivities," says Onkala. And with that he leaves with his escorts, joyfully acknowledging everyone that he encounters.

Sammiel takes this opportunity for solitude and re-enters his chambers. There he actually finds himself exhausted and tumbles onto his bedding. In no time at all he falls into a deep slumber. But it is an unnatural sleep. If one were to witness him sleeping, you would find his closed eyes dancing to and fro. For in his sleep state, he is restless and uneasy, all for good reason. It is during this time that Sammiel finds himself confronted by familiar surroundings. He is standing in and an open plain. The skies are ominously dark and rapidly rolling clouds speed above his head. Winds push the grass of the plains, yet he is untouched. Sammiel is steadfast and draws from within, the strength to face whatever is in his path. He takes in the scenery and sounds of this event and asks, "Who is it that dares to come upon me?"

Carried on the back of the wind, a voice rings out. "Sammiel….Sammiel my son." The stone of a man now suddenly softens and his eyes relax from their steely stare to that of a wide-eyed child. For….before him stands Manyara, his mother. It is the first time in a long time that Sammiel gives way to his emotion. His first reaction is one that is not expected of a man of his ruthlessness. He runs to his mother and tries to embrace her…..but it is for not. "I am but a specter of the image that you most remember my son," says Manyara. "But fear not, for I am truly here with you and we are here by my doing." "But how can this be mother? You are dead! Although I still mourn your loss, I presided over your burial ceremony." "Still your mind my son! You know the ways of your mother. I will never leave you. But now you must listen to me and understand what I am about to tell you." Manyara's voice is eerily calm and haunting. But she has succeeded in gaining Sammiel's attention.

"You have done well my son. You have taken your destiny into your own hands and are now master of your own fate. But you must ensure that you complete the task. Before you can lay claim to the throne and have the people to truly follow you. You must complete the ceremony of the Kings! Return to our homeland and assemble the shrines of the Kings. You must complete this in order for you to receive the gift," says Manyara. "What shrines and why must I give any merit to those pompous rotting corpses?" "SILENCE!" commands Manyara. As she speaks, something moves from beneath her. Something in what appears to be liquid form. But it is black and shimmers. It gives the appearance of being alive. Sammiel is not moved by this. He stands as if he is expecting it. The liquid continues toward him and soon makes contact. It begins to climb from his feet and moves intently upward. "You are behaving as a child! These steps must be taken to ensure your rightful place as king," instructs Manyara. "You will take a woman that you will soon encounter, as your wife. You will not harm her for she will be your ally and asset," she says. "Remember this and do so," commands Manyara. As she fades away, Sammiel stands for a brief moment encased in evil liquid form from his mother. And he awakes!

Darkness… a calmness all around. No sky, no earth to be found. There is no sound. The darkness seems to be endless. There is nothing or no one present, save for Numair. There is a brief nothingness and then he is soon encircled by flames that do him no harm. Distorted figures begin to approach from every direction. He is not afraid for he has experienced this before. Numair expects his father and grandfather, but who are the others that accompany them? Numair's questions are soon answered but not as he presumed. "Numair. You are more impressive than I had imagined," says one of the figures. "I am Lobengula; I am the first in our family line. Your destiny and those who will follow you exist because of the life that I lived and the belief of the people in our family. Everyone present belongs to our family. We make the essence of the Panther, the source of our power. Each of us is a fallen king, queen, princess, or prince from the chosen family. When we pass on to the ancestral plains, we are gathered together as one to strengthen the power of our gift," he continues.

Numair's heart is filled with pride to know this about his family. He is in awe of the multitude of family members surrounding him. The new king can feel their essence coursing through his body! He is different. The energy that flows through his body is powerful and pure.

Lobengula again speaks, "Numair, listen carefully young one. Your power of this gift is not complete and will not be until you have completed the task of kings."

"I do not understand this task, great one. What must I do to complete this task?" asks Numair.

"I will not deceive you, this will be a difficult quest for you," Lobengula tells him. "You must return to our homeland and enter the Chamber of the Kings. You must retrieve the royal headdress, shield, and weapons of your father and grandfather. Once you have these things you must construct their ancestral thrones. This is most difficult because you must face a troubling decision and foe. You will not gain the full power of our gift if you cannot accomplish this quest. If you are successful, you will be the one and true member of this family to receive the gift. Do you understand the significance of your destiny, young one?"

"I do, great one," is Numair's answer!

"Take the lessons and skills that you and the people witness here in this new land, back to assist in the creation of a new nation."

As Lobengula finishes the "Great Gathering", Numair watches as each member of the great ancestral family fades into the darkness. Until he is once again alone.

The dawn is once again upon Numair with the grueling training conducted by his teacher Kang. They spar in hand-to-hand combat. Numair bests him at every turn, so they move to weapons. Kang has introduced several of his native weapons. A multitude of hand-held, throwing, and long spear weapons. Numair's favorite weapon is the small and easily concealed rope dart. With this weapon he finds his mark with every strike. Teacher Kang displays a rare moment of approval. Their time together has built a bond between teacher and pupil. Kang has told of his coming to be aboard that horrid ship and in the midst of that unscrupulous crew. Kang hails from a land known as China. He says that it is one of the oldest nations on earth. He was a member of an exploration vessel. As the captain of the security detail, Kang was tasked to provide security for the explorers.

It was during a voyage of discovery to a curious land, at the time Kang and his people called the "Dark Lands" that Kang had received orders to lead a detachment of security for a mission of great discovery and vital importance. They were to search for a fabled source of indestructible nature. Their vessel arrived in an isolated cove of the "Dark Land" under the cover of night. The sky is a blanket of darkness, as no stars are out that night. A perfect cover for their arrival. As the crew prepared to make land at dawn, three mysterious vessels surrounded and attacked the anchored vessel. The mysterious ships boarded the lone vessel and a fierce battle ensued. The marauders launched an attack brandishing razor-sharp swords that slashed and maimed the crew members. Their numbers were great against the small crew of the exploration vessel. And the intent of the attackers was obvious. Kill everyone onboard! Kang quickly called his men to ranks to provide protection for the explorers, who he had hastened to their quarters below deck. As the attackers swarmed through the crew and made their approach towards the remaining survivors, Kang and his detachment launched their counter attack. The detachment's fighting style was something that these men of the west had never seen before. The precision of these fighters began to cut through the would-be attackers with ease. The hand-to-hand fighting and the strange weapons from the east startled the murderous attackers. The calm waters began to run red with the blood of the battle. The moment was beginning to favor Kang and his men. Their skill of the martial arts was profound. The detachment of security was easily dispatching the attackers and victory seemed imminent. But Kang suddenly hears the screams of death. He whirls around to his rear to view the source of the screams, simultaneously slashing one of the attackers' throats. The party for which he and his men were to protect are in the grasp of the enemy. Kang shouts to his men to cease the fighting. He is horrified and angered at what he witnesses. The band of explorers are in the grasp of the attackers. Bodies lay convulsing in response to their mortal wounds and answering the call of death.

Although angered Kang holds his ground. For in the clutches of the attackers' leader, held with a blade to his throat and on his knees is the head of the expedition… Kang's younger brother! Kang's startled reaction exposed the importance of the held hostage. It was at this very moment that Kang learns the name of his most hated foe. "Captain Hawkins, this one is special to him sir," states one member of the attacking horde. Kang was a scholarly man and understood the language of the attackers. He commanded that the hostages be released. "Throw down your weapons" was the reply from Captain Hawkins! "Surrender or they all die," he repeats. What seemed to be an eon, was only a brief moment. Kang's brother pleaded with him not to follow the instructions, but was met by a blunt strike to his face with the hilt of the sword of Captain Hawkins. As a show of his intent, Captain Hawkins orders the death of another explorer with just the motion of his hand. As one would expect, Kang is outraged and is in the midst of launching his attack, when his brother is clutched ever tighter. Kang has to restrain himself and orders his men to lower their weapons.

Hesitantly they do as their commander ordered. The henchmen quickly gather up the weapons and usher the Chinese warriors together. Once it became evident that Kang and his men were no longer a threat, the slaughter began. Kang surveyed the scene and immediately became aware of the reality of the what was to come. With the swiftness of the wind, Kang lunged forward attempting to reach his comrades, but he was unable to stop the mayhem that was to occur. The men in the back of the detachment were skewered from behind. Blades slash at the Chinese warriors before they could react. However, Kang and a few others are skilled in hand-to-hand combat and can defend themselves. Yet Kang is focused on reaching his brother. But Hawkins and a few henchmen leave the ship during the slaughter. Kang is enraged and fighting like a madman. He is outnumbered and weaponless, but men fall dead during his pursuit. He reaches aft of the ship, but Hawkins has fled. There is no time to take in what is happening, his men slaughtered and nowhere to retreat. Kang leaps into the darkness of the sea. It is the events from this night that has set Kang on his journey to find his brother and seek out his revenge on Captain Hawkins.

The revelation from Kang brings with it not only a kinship, but lessons of focus and determination. During a break, Kang takes away from his normal demeanor. "Young king, soon we will part ways. Before that time, I believe that you should have the men of your tribe begin training with us. We both have our quests to fulfill. Remember this, the powers that you have been granted are powerful weapons and must not be used for evil. But understand that you will have to face difficult choices in your quest to reclaim your family's kingdom and help your people. You will need the aid of fighters. The king himself cannot engage in battle alone. You must enlist the aid of others to have any chance of completing your task. Think about how you must and will go about your task of accomplishing this life mission before you," says Kang.

They continue the morning's training with a deeper intensity well into sunrise. The very next morning all of the men who were held captive alongside the young prince joined in their training. This routine was followed every day since that revealing conversation and, in time, Numair's army became proficient, tactical and deadly. Time is fleeting and they are progressing, but what is the expectation if they are to remain in this place? Although it has sheltered and protected their people, it is not their home.

At the insistence of a staunch supporter, they were ultimately placed with a benefactor, Lady Rebecca Protten, in the sea village of Yoruba. She is a handsome woman and very spirited. She has every captive of that horrid ship exposed to new skills and learning. The people are introduced to reading and writing. Surprisingly after several months, the people easily adapt to the teachings. This inspires Lady Protten to expand the lessons. She has men and women studying the arts, apprenticing architecture, sciences, and math. In a few years the people, specifically king Numair, develop a thirst for knowledge. Numair's zest for the unknown is vast and insatiable. She believes that it will ensure growth for all men to bridge the great divide of knowledge. Filled with excitement of Numair and his people's hunger for knowledge, Lady Protten often insists that the young king and the other children of the people spend time being children. She understands the hardships and horrors that the children have witnessed. She, regardless of the current climate of the times, would allow the children time to just run, laugh and play. More often than not, king Numair would take a bit more persuasion than the other children. He bore the tremendous weight of responsibility of his people. A fact that Lady Protten felt needed to balance. It was a matter that did not come immediately. After several persuasive conversations with the queen mother and grandmother, everyone agreed to improving the quality of life for all and especially the children. If only measured as a grain of sand in time, it would give joy to them and a sense of freedom. A sentiment that is not shared with many. The many different pale men from all corners of the world. They would see the tribal people being utilized in other areas. The concept of selling Numair's people as slaves or used for blood sport would quench their evil thirst. Or even worse, take their finest women and have their way with them and sell the use of their bodies for the pleasures of men or be mutilated and their body parts sold as exotic aphrodisiacs or medicinal remedies that only the wealthy could afford because of the rarity of them. But Lady Rebecca will have none of those horrid acts. She is a bright and clever woman. She accomplishes these lessons and much more, under the guise of using slaves as helpers to build a new compound for the benefit and glory of these strange peoples' "God". But the residents on the outside are suspicious and curious. On one occasion, while shopping at the market in town. Lady Rebecca along with Numair's grandmother and mother who have charge of the staff, along with Numair, were the intended targets to be accosted by two drunken seafarers. Lady Rebecca and the women were engaged in their dealings with a merchant. They did not notice the two scallions approaching from among all of the hustle and bustle of the street movement. But Numair noticed and quickly took action. In his arms were several packages, he concealed his intent, by calling out to Lady Rebecca and feigning a stumble and knocking into the two would-be attackers. While in the midst of the "accident", he spun one attacker about so swiftly that the force of the spin caused him to assault his companion. The two low-brow waifs began to argue amongst themselves and eventually engaged in fisticuffs among themselves. Numair welcomed the chance to inspect the two potential assassins hiding knives. The commotion startled Lady Rebecca, who quickly ushered the group back to the compound for safety. Not knowing the danger that she herself just avoided. Albeit it disappointed Numair, because his adventure had been interrupted. This has always been a treat for Numair. For since their arrival to this land, he has marveled at the many different structures that resembled a migrating herd of animals. For example, the first time that he saw glass. Numair stood in the center of the walkways and marveled at how the structures seem to stare at him… no one else, just him. He could not comprehend how these people were able to compel water to stop movement and stand in place for them. The more amazing portion of this wonder water, is that if you come close to it, one could see one's own reflection! But the marvel did not cease at that point, no. He would advance even closer and by all of the stars, he could see within the structures! There are walking patterns strewn about through the township. There is no grass to soften the steps. The air is foul from the smell of dead fish and tainted sea water from the refuse of human waste most days. Others are salty and mixed with the smells of the strange food of this land. Everyone dresses strange here. The garments range from dirty and tattered to beautiful layers of fine material that is soft to the eye and the touch. But the clothes that he has been expected to wear itch. Upon reflection, none of the men ever fully felt comfortable in their new garb. Yet the worst of all of the new land belongings are these torture items called shoes! They bind your feet and have no flexibility. How can they enjoy mother earth with these stifling and unwavering wood and animal hide bindings? Upon their return to the compound, Numair gave instructions to all that she,

(Lady Rebecca), must never be left unguarded. But also avoid her being aware of our protective intent. We must be vigilant at all times and safeguard our benefactor, commands Numair. They all know that they must make good use of their time here as well as their new learned skills. Numair is determined that they will not become permanent additions to these lands.

The encounter with the scoundrels in the market place did not go unnoticed. Quite the opposite. It is the respect of Lady Rebecca that most of the shopkeepers and local workers are calmed and reasoned with. Her gentle nature and kindness has earned her a sort of protection from the local business owners and those who have benefited from her generosity. But the local riff-raff gather together in a dimly lit hovel of a room. The consensus through the room is hatred for the Africans! It has however been some time since the incident. But the very existence of the free people of the compound incites the low-brow drunkards of the township. Without actual slights against them, personal harm or even property taken from them, this band of zealots only want to hate and harm those who are different from them. So suggestion to trash the interlopers and teach them subordination is greeted with exuberant cheers. The decision is made to attack the compound under the cover of darkness. Believing that this would lend to the element of surprise as well as keep their identities hidden.

At dusk the plan is set into motion. Small teams of ragged men scuttled through alleyways and dark corridors leading out of the township, twelve in all. There is no apparent leader amongst them. But there are instigators throughout. They are armed with fish hooks and harpoons from their various ships. Some have sailor's cutlasses and others are armed with simple rusty daggers. Scuttling through the darkness, the men can see the compound just outside of the township to the south. Once they feel is a sufficient distance from the prying eyes of would-be do-gooders, the mob assembles to make a hasty coordinated plan of attack.

One of the vermin insists that they proceed on the side of caution, but the more aggressive members hastily silence him by berating him and challenging his commitment to this endeavor. A hulking example of a man, goes so far as to insist that the Africans are weak and inferior and that the men will more than likely offer their women and children in exchange for their lives. And it would seem that this is the consensus among this ragtag band of marauders. The dense fog from the sea has rolled inland, and the moon offers little light, but rather transforms shadows into eerie figures. The scoundrels contend that this will lend to further their cause. So the men press on with heightened anticipation of their conceived victory this night. Many have succumbed to underestimating an opponent that they deem inferior to their forces. This night is no different!

The young tribal king Numair has become aware of the interlopers. He is ever vigilant and is beginning to master his keen abilities. He could hear the men rumbling through the town and villains never seem to know to be silent. Numair's vision has watched the approaching thugs from the onset of their intentions. He has gathered his trained warriors and positioned them in strategic locations throughout the compound also along the path that the would-be attackers have chosen. All that remains is the command to strike. Although untested in battle with a military force, Numair is surprisingly calm and patient. He allows the intruders to advance further into the snare. He too prefers to keep the township clueless as to the impending events to come. He knows that none can be spared to possibly give cause for an even greater retaliation.

His surreal engagement with Kang has birthed the realization that blood must be spilled along this journey in order to achieve victory in regaining the kingdom and freeing the people. He has embraced fate.

The overconfident attackers make their way farther away from the township and deeper into Numair's ambush. Bumbling footsteps step on and break fallen twigs and leaves. Chatter and glowing lanterns illuminate the attacking party like an open window. Just as the township disappears over the horizon, Numair stealthily lowers himself from his position high among the treetops behind the advancing party. He makes himself known by simply asking the men of their intentions. His inquiry is met by foul language and vicious postures. The brave cowards are just about to advance upon the lone African, when Numair halts their progress with a hand gesture. Conversation over. Firmly in place, he signals for the ground troops to make themselves known. Just beyond the tree line, the small valleys throughout the landscape provide excellent cover for the hidden troops. Long grass and the cover of darkness, the little moonlight along with the lanterns of the inept mob, lend for a horrifying night. Rising up through the fog from their positions, Numair's men appear as monstrous demons from the bowels of hell to the mentally limited mob.

It is but a brief moment of silence, but that hesitation seemed an eternity for the ill-fated group. With the cry of "shambulizi," it begins. Powerful Numair simply walks from behind the would-be murderers and proceeds to grasp a man by his forehead and chin… snap! The ease and swiftness of the act is undetected by the others within the group. Numair's men move in formations of precision and directness. Groups of three warriors would take to one attacker and proceed to attack different sectors of the body. A swift and damaging kick to the leg joint, simultaneously another warrior thrusts a powerful rib-shattering blow that doubles their opponent over. The final warrior lands the death blow with a precision kick to either the temple region of the head or, if the warrior is truly skilled, before the opponent could bend at the knee or double over in pain from the other warriors. This warrior heel-kicks his victim firmly in the neck and breaks it.

The attackers panic and scatter in every direction. And that seals their fate. Tactically placed throughout the area, Numair's men make short work of each of the remaining mob members without mercy. Numair orders the warriors to transport the bodies, weapons, lanterns, and anything giving evidence of the skirmish. The area is cleared of the bodies and tools are used to work the land to the very edge of the township's borders. To the average person, it would seem as though the men from the township simply vanished just as they reached the edge of the township. The bodies were gathered up and transported in hasty slings and spirited away to a remote cliff edge that is littered with jagged rocks and crashing waves. The bodies are tossed over the high edge and washed away to sea. The distance is far, but the sturdy warriors of Numair run the trek without pause. Numair and his men return to their quarters and everyday activities. Numair does not show any signs of wavering under the scrutiny of the local officials' search of the compound and questioning of Lady Rebecca. The investigation, searches, and constant interrogations carry on for weeks. Although they may have their suspicions, the local law dismisses the people of the compound as perpetrators of any heinous crimes. They view them as weak in physical attributes and mental capabilities. Numair has overcome a major milestone in his journey.

Weeks have passed since the incident, but all investigations have surrendered nothing from the compound or the residents. The disappearance of the men of the township has heightened tensions against the compound and the foreigners of this continent. The fact that young Numair, although heavily burdened with responsibility, is still yet a child, does not go unnoticed by the queen mother. There are moments away from the strain of day-to-day activities, that she and her mother would spend bonding moments alone with the young king. In those moments, royal duties, the current situation, nor the tasks that lay ahead are discussed. Instead, the history and legends of old are explored. The nature of their being is taught to the young king. This is to assist Numair in knowing who he is and where he and his people come from. And to instill the knowledge and pride of belonging to a long ancestry of accomplished people with the understanding that moving forward can only be accomplished successfully by adhering to the lessons and knowledge of the past.

Numair seeks counsel from their wisest and most revered people. He seeks counsel from his mother and grandmother. After the day has settled and all have taken quarters for the night, they meet at the rear of the compound. He often confers with them for guidance or reassurance. But this conversation is of a different nature. Difficult decisions must be formulated and decided upon.

"My son, you seem troubled, and the urgent nature of your request to meet causes worry upon me," asks his mother, Adero.

"I agree," interjects his grandmother, Akilah.

"I feel the time is near for our people to begin our journey back to our homeland and begin anew," he tells them.

"Thank the ancestors," states his grandmother. "But I sense you have an issue with an immediate departure."

"I must agree with you, my child. Our time with these people has been fruitful, but we are not of this land or culture," she states.

"And you must ensure that our people are prepared for the long and dangerous journey," adds my mother.

"What are your concerns, Numair?" she asks.

"We have been among our saviors for some time now," he begins. "Our time here has allowed our people to come to understand and prosper from our exposures. From our language exchange, we gained such vast knowledge and cultural understandings. Some of our people have grown fond of this strange land and begun new families. Some of those wish to remain here and begin new lives. The training that I have instituted among our people, although for protection. Some have fire for blood and wish to do harm to those who have transgressed against us. We have now been away from our beloved homeland for nine years. I have searched deep within and feel that the time is very near for our departure," he confides to them.

"Then it is simple, my son," his mother says. "You will gather your people and tell them to begin preparation for the long journey," she says.

"Your people love and believe in you, Numair," says grandmother. "But these matters are trivial, child. There is something deeper that torments you. Come now, tell us what troubles your heart, young king?"

Here in this moment, he confesses his dilemma. The years of their journey to this point, now finds not Numair the clever young boy. In his place stood a tall, roughed and muscular young man. He is handsome yet intense. He gives his audience his full attention. He proceeds to explain the conflict of facing his uncle Sammiel and the need to retake the throne and restore the kingdom. Numair cannot fathom that the love and the cherished memories of his life before, were all a lie! He tells them that his heart is heavy from the daunting task that he must complete. He tells them of his past struggles to contain his anger. Of how he came to understand his transformation and how the elders advised him to calm his heart and mind. He told of the moment a few years ago, that he began to see the world differently from his previous perception. He knows that this is what was causing the delay in his decision to take the people home, he bares all to the women in his life.

"You are the king!" Queen Akilah sternly states. Her eyes take on the familiar steely stare. "I understand your hesitation or rather the fear that grips you. But I am telling you! You are stronger than the fear that grips you or the doubt that you seek to hide behind. You know the only choice here. Besides, I long to feel the sun from my home upon my flesh again. I dream of the sweet taste of the water from 'my' river. You can take comfort in the knowledge that we, your people, will be beside you every step of the way and even into battle when the time comes, and my child, it will come and you will be victorious! Now prepare to lead your people to glory and get out of your own way! I will not speak of this again. You are the king and I will not remind you again." And with that, grandmother gave him a lash to his head and walked away.

With only his mother as a springboard for his thoughts, Numair posed the same issues to her again. But being a woman of their nation, she too gave him the sound and definite defiance as his grandmother. "We do not belong here!" she says. "Yes, some of the people here have been kind to us, but this is not our home. We must return and reclaim what was taken from us and have those who have offended our family and people suffer the wrath of vengeance. I speak not as your mother, but as a member of your people, my king. Take us home!"

The council has concluded and his purpose is clear. They both adjourn to their quarters and no other words are spoken. Numair no longer has reservations and his thoughts are focused. The next morning Numair sends word via the trainees, to have the people meet this night at this gathering point. During the course of the day, he decided to speak to Lady Rebecca, they owe a great gratitude to her, and he feels compelled that she must be made aware of his decision and he cares for her. She asks him to escort her to market and that they should have their discussion along the way. He agrees and they make arrangements to do so. As the carriage leaves the confines of their place of sanctuary, Lady Rebecca takes Numair by surprise by addressing him as "your highness!"

"It was not difficult to see how you are treated by your people," she says as she laughs. "Gathering from your desire to speak with me, you have come to the decision to take your people home. Would that be a correct statement?" she asks. He gathers himself as she has completely astounded the young king.

"Your observation is correct, my lady," he tells her. "You have been a beacon of salvation for us. We owe you so much. I am, however, also concerned for your safety in our absence. Some of my people have come to embrace the way of life here and have asked to remain behind and continue their lives among the people of the township. I wanted to assure you that they will continue to keep your safety in the forefront," he says.

She now is the one who is surprised as Numair continues to explain to her the events from weeks and months past. Visibly shaken by the revelation of the news of danger to her being. But after she gathers her senses, he continues to explain to her of the training of some of the men and women who have chosen to stay behind with her. Years later Lady Rebecca became a beloved and devoted missionary and evangelist. Her work makes an indelible mark in history.

As they continue their day, off in the distance a familiar figure has just been released from the confines of imprisonment. It is an old familiar foe, the fat grizzled captain from their initial vessel of imprisonment. He has caught sight of Numair and stays in the shadows, but keeps a vigil upon the pair's presence. Numair can sense him and his smell is distinctive. But he proceeds without acknowledging his presence. He is of no significance nor does he pose a threat. But Numair cannot forgo the opportunity to pester him. As they approach one shop through the heavy crowd of people, Numair momentarily blends into the crowd and makes his way to the rooftops. He spies his target as he walks along the roof of another shop, he does not notice the array of seagulls fluttering away from Numair's approach. The birds are of many in number and one of the first things that young Numair noticed upon their arrival to this township. Numair quietly eases his way down the side of the building and slowly approaches from his rear. The captain is focused on Lady Rebecca's location, but unaware of their exact position. Slightly bent forward with head and eyes straight ahead, Numair pats his back with noticeable force as he excuses himself past him. As he does so, Numair briefly turns to face him as he walks past him. The act frightens him so that he cannot restrain himself from shrieking from fear. Numair continues back to Lady Rebecca's side as the inept spy runs off in the other direction. Lady Rebecca and Numair continue their conversation. They discuss many topics. One of which is the completion of the compound before Numair and his people take leave on their journey. The compound is comprised of two large buildings and several smaller buildings. One of the larger buildings is used for gathering on what Lady Rebecca calls Sunday service. This is a very sacred place for Lady Rebecca as well as some of the people from the township. Numair and his people greatly respect this particular building for it is the one place that all people gather together no matter what the color of their skin. It has always fascinated him for all of the rich colors and grand figures made of wood and precious metals. During his first encounters, he could not enjoy all of the sights and sounds that this place had to offer because of the itchy clothing and stiff foot coverings that they were required to wear. Grandmother would always pinch him if he moved about too much, trying to see all of the sights and different people in attendance. And mother would always usher him to assist the loud and seemingly angry man who was called the "Reverend". But, despite all of this, Numair always enjoyed this day. He had very little chores to attend to and the meals on the days that they would all gather were always delicious. With so much time in this place, they have come to know the special occasions of the people of this land as well as the visitors from other countries. Numair especially enjoyed the one called "Christmas". Although he is now the king of his people, he was still a child that is growing into manhood, he loved to receive the gifts that the day would bring. For some time he did not know why they would receive them, but nonetheless, he greatly anticipated this one day.

The other large building was the great hall of study. Here Lady Rebecca has established the primary building of a school. The administration and library were housed as well as a gathering point for important meetings. There are several smaller buildings that Lady Rebecca has commissioned as classrooms. Here they are exposed to the arts, Latin and other languages, mathematics, engineering, and sciences. Lady Rebecca reveals to Numair that it has been her vision that one day the compound will become a great Mecca of higher learning. And Numair intends to ensure that she sees that vision to fruition. Further inside the compound, near the rear wall, are the living quarters. Here they have some semblance of a home. Families are once again whole and under one roof. It gives all a sense of pride to have their own place of sanctuary. Lady Rebecca wants to see the grounds expand and incorporate even more to her vision of learning. There are also several other buildings among the living quarters. One of the houses stored foods. Another is used for the residents of their temporary home to gather for all of their meals to eat and cook. Two more buildings round out the compound. There is a large building with six stalls to house these animals called horses. They are beautiful and majestic. But the inside smells very awful, and Numair has the task to assist in the upkeep. Not one of his favorite duties. But nothing is more demeaning or smells as bad as the last building… it's where the people of these lands like to go to release their excrements. It is a long building with wooden boxes that rest over a large hole in the ground. There a large container is used to catch the foul-smelling body ejections, whether one is making water or something else. The duty of clearing the containers falls upon those who do not follow the rules of the compound or are found to be of no other use… awful. Finally, there is the wall that encompasses the entire compound. It is near completion and has a lookout tower in each corner of the complex. Lady Rebecca has requested assistance to complete the wall and to help install a large gate of some kind to ensure the safety of the residents once Numair and his people have departed. Of course he agrees, for she has been nothing but kind to all of his people since their rescue from the dark and murky grip from the long river, now known as the sea. In return, Lady Rebecca will supply their traveling needs as well as medicines and maps to assist in the journey back to their lands. It is agreed that all will be completed and they depart in two months. But Numair is not completely comfortable departing without knowing who was behind the last attempt upon Lady Rebecca. After some thought, Numair decided to investigate and put an end to any plot before they depart.

A few nights shortly thereafter, Numair waited for full darkness to fall before he slipped out of the compound undetected. Or so he thought. Upon Numair's descent from the compound wall, he turned and came face to face with Kang. He stands sternly and motionless. "Bold young king," he says. "Do you really think that you should do this with your face exposed?" With that he turns to a stored bag he has placed underneath a bush. From the bag he retrieves clothing. "These are the garments of spies from the east," he says. "They go by the name of Ninja, from a land near my own that is hailed as Japan. Their assassins use the cover of darkness and these garments to cover their deeds. We will wear these to cover our identities."

"Ours?" Numair asks with dismay.

"Yes, ours, young king," he replies! "Did you think I would allow you to go on this journey without your final lessons in stealth? Now please make haste and prepare for your lessons," he urges.

They don the apparel and Numair has hesitation to adorn the headpiece. But a smack on the back of the head from Kang helps him to decide to wear it. He is covered in black cloth with a hood for his head. It is a bit large for him, so he fashions holes for his eyes. Kang hands him the final piece of the attire. They are like spear tips, but are arranged to fit into the palm of one's hand by way of a ribbon that is tied around the entire hand. It feels appropriate. A bit loose fitting for Numair, but Numair will make adjustments to his taste at a more opportune time.

Once finished they head for the township. Kang is fast enough to keep pace with him, but soon takes the lead as he has his suspicions as to who is behind the plot. Quietly and undetected they head towards the wharf district. There many seafarers take refuge in some of the seedier establishments. Down the dark and filthy break between the structures, they quickly head up to the rooftops. Kang falls slightly behind as Numair effortlessly makes his way up the side of the structure, Kang does not possess Numair's abilities, but gives him a pat on the back once he joins him up top. Together they spend many nights searching and listening for any hint of who the perpetrators are, but nothing. That is until one fateful night they scout a small group of miscreants making their way to a familiar dark and foreboding ship. There is no moon or stars out this night. The waters of the sea are as black as soot from a burned cauldron. It is a hated slave ship. It did not go down into the dark murky depths of the sea it would seem. Numair's blood begins to boil! Numair's gift takes form throughout his body. But he remains focused and presses on. They scale the ship and Numair makes his way along the side of the ship. A group of men are gathered in conference there. Numair can hear their conversation and does not like what he hears.

"We do not have to go and put ourselves in danger, when we have a well-stocked supply of dark savages ripe for the picking in that blasted compound!" one voice shouts. "We only have to get past that lonely woman standing in our way."

Another voice, a more commanding and direct voice, gave the final word to attack and take Numair's family by force and hinted that it would be of no consequence if Lady Rebecca were a victim of the attack. Harsh words and even more harsh was the act itself. They could not allow this to happen. Numair and Kang laid in wait until they emerged topside before they launched their attack. Suddenly and without warning storm clouds roll in. The mood is instantly changed. Kang tosses down smoke bombs to blind the riff-raff. From there the pair begin their assault. They bound from the sides of the dark ship, Numair is pleased to place two well-placed kicks to the faces of these filthy animals. From the kicks he bounds into a delightful flip and spin to sweep the legs from three more. The deck is hard but slippery from the constant sea spray and slime. Kang engages a small band of thralls, but his attack is mortal in nature. Kang is fighting with a vengeance and unbridled anger! Numair cannot give pause to question him, so he fights on. Before everyone is dead, Numair takes the ringleader into custody. He cripples him by breaking his legs and arms with two swift moves. He poses no threat now. Numair grasps him by his hair as he squirms in agony.

"Coward! Why hide behind a mask?" he asks. He does not see my face! Perfect! Numair begins by questioning him as to why he and his men persist in their pursuit of Lady Rebecca.

"With her removed we can harvest all of those dark walking pieces of silver she protects," he states.

As Numair turns to Kang for his thoughts, he notices all of the dead men strewn about the deck. Time paused, frozen in that moment. An eerie finger of lightning reaches from the heavens and touches the sea, Numair whirls in search of Kang only to hear a gasp near his position. As he turns his focus to the captive, he finds Kang holding the scoundrel by the hair with his throat slit! With the light of the lightning strike behind him. Kang simply takes his leave and Numair can only follow. Although he is shaken, they do not speak. Just as quickly as they came, the storm clouds simply fade away. They slip back into the night and the compound without any illumination. There is a brief investigation into the deaths of the discovered seafarers. The constable and his men come to the compound, but conclude that "the dark people" are too dim-witted to have committed such a heinous and calculated crime. And that Kang, who never speaks to anyone, save for Numair and his inner circle, is too small and frail to have any part of this mass murder. Once again, they are just "those people of the compound" and eliminated from suspicion.

The final week of their stay in the township is strangely a sad occasion. Kang and Numair meet early for their final training. But Kang is not dressed for training. Instead he has his belongings packed and has arranged for them to meet alone. He goes on to give Numair his final advice.

"Young king," he begins. "You will do many great things in the days to come in your life. But there is this task that you cannot avoid nor turn from when the time comes. When you engage in battle with the one who has harmed your family, the only choice that you have… is that you must kill him! I know it will be difficult and heart-wrenching, but unless this deed is done, he will most certainly kill you and then your entire family and all who support you."

Numair knows what he is saying is true, and he promises that he will not fail. They embrace one another and Numair asks his teacher and friend for one last favor. Kang agrees before anything else can be said. Numair asks him to allow a small band of ten men who wish to continue to train with him, to join him on his quest. After a few moments of thought, Kang agrees to the request. Upon their return to the compound, the entire inhabitants of the compound give a joyous and heartfelt farewell to Kang. He has become a member of their family. The men join Kang and they depart.

A few days later it is the main party that now departs. They are leaving at this time due to the insistence of Numair's mother. She did not want to leave until she received a sign. Her reasoning is sound, but cumbersome. All are anxious to begin, but the respect she commands, no one will question her. Even Numair dares not do so. Finally she made a decision which is this day! Lady Rebecca has provided three oxen-drawn carts complete with rations for several months. She has also included sleep covers and blankets. During their last few months together, Kang and Numair stockpiled weapons in preparation for the defense of the convoy. They all gather together in the compound square and give their farewells. It is the crest of dawn when they make their final departure from the compound. The journey home has begun and the feeling among the people is one of excitement and longing for a return to paradise.

CHAPTER 8

Evil Stands Alone

With the celebration in full regalia, many are not interested in the festivities. Instead, combative conversations are taking place.

"Why would you want to attack yet another village so soon?" asks Onkala. "We have only just returned victorious from our last campaign!"

"We are conquerors whose only quest should be to rule all of the lands!" replies Sammiel.

"That is not what we agreed to," retorts Onkala angrily. "We were to overthrow your family's lands and rule jointly! My people are now prosperous and happy. We have a future before us now and see a greater standard of life for the first time," states Onkala. "Why must we upset the calm of the waters when we have everything that we have ever dreamed of?"

"Then your dreams are small and simple," shouts Sammiel. "This is nothing compared to the future that I plan to build! You and your simple people will join me in this conquest of all of the lands. Everything will be under one rule!"

"And just who will be ruler of this large and mighty land?" asks Onkala.

A snap of his head and an intense stare from Sammiel is the first reaction to the posed question. But after a brief moment to gather his thoughts, Sammiel responds.

"Why, I am simply pointing out that we are in this together, dear friend and ally," states Sammiel. "We both envisioned ruling the lands equally, correct, and we agreed to start with the overthrowing of my father's kingdom. I am merely stating that now that we have the opportunity to do so, why not expand our thinking and realm?"

An awkward silence stifles the air. Two pairs of eyes burn with rage. Shadows from the fires seem to form two combatants that dance with each flicker. As the fire grows with each tiny gust of wind, no matter how small, the dance grows in intensity. That changes when one figure starts to outdo the other. It gives the appearance that one completely engulfs the opposition.

The silence is once again broken by Onkala. "Of course we are united in our quests," says Onkala. "Let us not bicker over trivialities. Have you a march in mind? Or perhaps we could divide our forces and attack two subjects simultaneously? What is your wish, Almighty Sammiel?" asks Onkala, obviously in a mocking tone.

Visibly perturbed with the conversation, Onkala grants a moment for a response, but decidedly gives his regards as he and others take their leave of the fireside meeting. Alone by the fire, Sammiel's face reflects the shadows of the flames, which oddly enough reflect his temperament at the current events. The shadow flames dance and contort in all different shapes and forms. Chaotic are the forms. Fierce and rhythmless, the fire and Sammiel's mind race. He can be seen motionless by the fire, but obviously deep in thought by all outward appearances.

But as the evening settles and the sounds of the night spread across the plains, there is nothing that can penetrate this moment. Eyes focused, devoid of all of his surroundings, it is as if Sammiel has gone into a state of slumber while standing. He does not notice the hot embers that crackle and fly from the fire, only to land near his feet. Nor does he acknowledge the large snake that has made its way into the camp and slithers quietly behind Sammiel, yet moves close enough to give the appearance of being in the company of kindred spirits. As it very well may be, for Sammiel's rigid body, although surrounded by the encampment of the village and hot earth beneath his feet, feels and reacts to nothing. In truth, Sammiel is in a deep conversation. A conversation with a heavy topic! For his spirit has been removed to another plane. One of which he is now familiar with. There he can be found to be conversing with his mother! Or so it would seem. Repeatedly, a whisper is heard by Sammiel, "KILL HIM, KILL HIM, KILL HIM!"

It has been an entire week of celebration and relaxation for the warring people that are led by two men, Onkala and Sammiel. A union that, by all appearances, was spawned from the darkest depths of evil and bloodlust. But the harmony of this partnership is not to be. On this morning, the sun gently caresses the treetop canopy and casts long fingers of light throughout the village and stretches across the landscape. Flowers burst with excitement as if to greet a precious loved one. The blades of grass stretch each stalk up as to form open arms to accept the warm embrace of mother sun. As life awakes, so does death. But it is cunning and silent. Deeds done in secret hold unspeakable treacheries. In the shadows of the morning, figures gather in the shadows.

"At the defeat of our newest targets, he dies," a voice states. "Then it is settled, it must be done for the prosperity of all."

Six runners, one from every direction, arrive at the village of the mighty conquerors of people. Stealthily runners approach less are known by the guards. The pounding sounds of running feet cause many to stir from slumber. They converge on the huge sitting area in the very center of the village. These men are tall, lean, and disciplined. They have the endurance of the Hyena and are just as deadly. They are known for being able to run at a constant pace for six days and still fight as fiercely as a fresh warrior. All were carrying and wearing weapons, small amounts of food, water, and shields. There they await. Immediately, a roar of a voice is so thunderous that it causes birds to take flight from their branches and nests!

"Why are you out and about?" shouts Onkala. His presence is sudden and mysterious, as he seems to just appear. He causes the men to swiftly turnabout in surprise. Although his question is rhetorical, he poses not this question. Yet the men are not his intended audience; he is seeking the presence of the one who can answer the actual questions that flood his mind and anger.

"I am the one you want to question, Onkala!" a powerful voice interjects. From the mist of the fading morning approaches Sammiel, just as mysteriously as Onkala.

"You did this for what purpose?" asks Onkala insistently.

"We agreed that we would continue to forge the land to further expand our budding empire, did we not?" impishly asks Sammiel.

Rage now paints Onkala's face. "So you and you alone will make decisions for everyone, including myself?" angrily asks Onkala.

"Why, on the contrary, my dear friend," states Sammiel. "Knowing all of the responsibilities that you have leading the people, I merely had your best interest at heart and decided to take one less worry from you," says Sammiel in a very condescending manner.

Placing his arm around Onkala, Sammiel leads him to the circle of men. "Come now, friend, let us hear of what is to be reported." This, for the time, brings Onkala's anger down to give him a calmer nature. Onkala is not a very good statesman, but he is a terrifying warrior. He leads by force, but the last few years have taught him lessons of diplomacy from his dealings with Sammiel. He succumbs and lends ear.

"What news have you warriors to report?" asks Sammiel. One by one, the men render their findings. All have news of distant villages, but only one sparks the interest of Sammiel. It is a village four days' march away. It contains riches and a large number of potential cargo for trading with the men of the sea.

"Away with you," commands Onkala. "Sammiel, shall we counsel?" asks Onkala. An approving nod from Sammiel and the two men come to an agreement to march upon the reported land of riches. Surprisingly, the two have a once again united mind in the planning of the attack. One could say that it was the calm before the storm. But nonetheless, that very morning all is planned out and ready for execution. Not only of the impending battle with the wealthy tribe, but there are underlying objectives planned out as well.

"The march will leave for victory in three days' time," the men agree. The days between will allow for any lingering wounds to heal and rest for the scouts. Supplies and weapons are made ready. And families will have, for some, their final times together. Thus are the final days of preparations.

Jewels are abundant above and below. The canvas of the night is littered with stars, and the tall grass of the plains is sprinkled throughout with the glowing eyes of animals piercing from the stalks in wonderment of the thundering sounds of the upright creatures that disturb the dark and early moments of the morning. Creatures they may be, they are merely the massive army commanded by Sammiel and Onkala. All are focused and steady in their march. The stars all seem to peer from the heavens to witness the spectacle that is to come. If any predators are out and about and in their path, they depart the area with haste as the massive march resembles a gigantic black snake slithering along a predetermined path and devouring all in its wake. To see this wondrous spectacle is awe-inspiring. In the distance, a pride of lions in the throes of a kill ceases all motion to view the massive dark beast make its way across country, and all bound away in fear. As the massive march fades into the distance, few families merely stand and watch until the march is no longer visible.

The high morning sun finds the massive march doubled in pace. Relentless is the march, unwavering and ground is devoured with each step. So powerful and swift is the march that it cuts a path along its course. For two days this continues until on the morning of the third day of marching, the massive army finally halts three leagues from its appointed destination.

"Rest," commands Sammiel. "For tonight, we march to victory and bathe in riches!" A controlled roar of the marching troops explodes out of the small oasis that has been chosen to be the campsite for the resting army.

"Eat and prepare yourselves for battle," interjects Onkala. "Sammiel, shall we go over final plans?" Again,

Sammiel renders his approval by way of a nod of his head. The two men find a secluded location and they too make preparations. It will be a two-pronged attack, coming from a frontal assault, while one will attack from a flanking position, preventing any retreat. Small bands will contain any attempts to flee to the east or the west. The two exchange forearm grasps in agreement and decide that Onkala will lead the frontal assault. From there, the only remaining matter is rest until the cover of darkness steals the stage from the day.

The choice to hurry the pace becomes clear. The darkness gives imagery of the eyes of the heavens being closed as this is a moonless night and there are no stars to give light to the events that are set to take place. As the hour of battle approaches, battle formations take positions. Two small units begin their descent towards their prospective locations. They are silent in their hastened march, but swift to reach their destination. It is a matter of hours before they make contact. It is the eastern unit that first encounters a band of sentries. They are only three men and are quickly dispatched. The first to fall is the runner, his assignment is to run back to the village and warn the others of approaching danger. He is swift of foot. But like a gazelle, a well-aimed throw of a spear fells him and he is dead. The other two attempt to engage, but the second to fall is a short but stout individual. He draws a blade and takes a fighting stance. But the enemy he faces is well versed in combat and quickly surrounds him and initiates an attack from the front to distract him. As he braces to take on the attackers, he disregards the attackers to his rear. A fatal mistake. He gets off one swing of his blade and a step… then his throat is cut. His lifeless body falls immediately to his knees and halts. His head can only dangle and rest on his back from the severity of the cut. Blood sprays the area and blankets the grass and people around him. The only one in this melee to be affected by this gruesome scene is the third sentry. He decides that he does not want to receive the same fate and drops to his knees with his hands to the sky in surrender. The unit leader gives a silent command to proceed forward, and the unit continues its march. The sentry begins to breathe a sigh of relief and quietly gives thanks for his life. But no chance can be taken on acquiring captives by the support units. So it is the last two attackers that each gorge the sentry with their long spears and proceed to push the spears deeper into the sentry until it becomes obvious that his life force has left this world. The blood from the speared body also sprays the landscape and the torsos and legs of the two executioners. They dislodge their weapons and survey the surroundings. Confident in the security, they rejoin the unit on the final approach. The west unit encounters the same obstacles as the east's. The sentries in this remote location meet the same fate as their brethren of the eastern sentry post. The two units reach their appointed locations in no time at all. Both attacking forces take up positions and await the impending battle.

It has been exactly one hour since the smaller units have begun their march into position. Now it is Sammiel and his warring command to move next. They are large in number and just as swift as the two smaller units. They are in fact much faster in their pace, for they must take the longest route to reach their destination. It is a spectacular display of precision as this massive force moves through the darkness without breaking a single branch or disturbing even the smallest pebble. They are a formidable force, and their prey will soon discover this. A wide path is the route to reach the attack point and they do with no resistance. The last to move into position are Onkala and his troops. Having waited for an additional hour, he moves his forces out. They march at a normal pace to allow Sammiel and his forces ample time to take their positions. His march is larger than that of Sammiel, but just as disciplined as his. The hour of blood is near. As the march of Onkala nears the edge of the village, they suddenly halt. The formation reveals itself by expanding to encompass the entire opening of the sleeping village. Onkala takes a few paces to the front of the encroaching army and surveys the landscape. He waits and listens.

And then it comes! It is a familiar shrill. One he has heard before. A smile crosses his face and his next words unleash death! And with those words, the roar of the frontal troops signals the unleashing of a night of horror to many and death to most. Shouts of alarm can be heard from some of the men of the village, but they are too late… the death toll begins.

The charge of the frontal assault is thunderous and vicious. The sleeping wildlife is startled from their slumber by the war cries! Some of the village men struggle to get their weapons and begin to defend their people, but some fall as they emerge from their quarters. Heads are bludgeoned and bodies are speared before a single weapon is raised. In the wake of this destruction, fires are set to force the residents out into the open. Many rush towards the brush and trees on the surrounding sides, but are met by the previously stationed attackers who hungrily await their prey. The warriors that pose the most immediate threat are slaughtered immediately by two and three marauders, seemingly from every direction. They stand no chance of victory and the remaining fleeing members realize this and surrender with no further resistance. They are shackled and gathered together in one area under the watchful eye of their captors. They are the lucky ones tonight. Back in the village, there is a different scenario taking place.

A lifeless body falls to the ground headless and covered in blood. His murderer wastes no time seeking out his next victim. A lone fighter is vanquishing two attackers when the murderer launches an attack from the rear. Only this time, his spear does not find its target. Instead of victory, the attacker is met by a long knife to his abdomen. The lone fighter is superior and rushes off to aid others of his village. In other areas of the battle, the scene is repeated as several warriors defeat the attacking forces and begin to band together and become even stronger.

Onkala, who is unaware of the events taking place, is reveling in the slaughter. He takes great pleasure in the battle itself. He runs to all encounters, seeking the rush of the act of combat. In doing so, he often loses himself to a bloodlust and goes into a maddening state of mind. He kills on instinct. A sword-wielding enemy runs towards him screaming a boisterous battle cry. Onkala unleashes his sword to meet the oncoming strike, repels it, and swings back to find the neck of his foe. But his blade is lodged between the neck and shoulder. Onkala is distracted for a moment as he vigorously attempts to dislodge his weapon. He does not notice that a small band of men have surrounded him. As he dislodges his weapon, he is struck with a glancing slice to his midsection. This is because he sensed the attack a moment just before the strike. He quickly surveys his predicament and settles himself for battle. He engages them with full bravado. A glorious battle ensues and Onkala rips through flesh with great relish. But he now realizes that he has been separated from his men and now stands totally alone.

Onkala is magnificent in his battle! He is constantly wounded from all sides, yet he fights on with little thought that his life will end for he is confident in his skills. But the fighting has brought the attention of other fighters and it soon becomes apparent that he will soon be overwhelmed. As Onkala continues to fight on, the village burns around him, but his men are being vanquished at every turn now. For what began as a simple overwhelm-with-numbers strategy now proves to be a grossly underestimated folly. The warrior Onkala worries not of these mere setbacks; instead, he continues to slaughter each opponent as they continuously attack him. Until one blow from his right is too overpowering in finding its target, that it sends Onkala to his right knee. He is weary now and contends himself to death… but he will not die kneeling! With every fiber of his being, Onkala rises to his feet with a powerful roar! And prepares to meet his glory with shield, blade, and spear. With every breath, he is assessing his fighting needs. And now he is ready. He charges a cluster of men with ferocity, only to be felled with countless blows. Blood oozing from his skull obscures his vision, but his pride will not allow him to give up the fight. Blurred sight be damned, Onkala valiantly steadies himself for the final battle on this plain.

He takes hold of his blade with both hands and again prepares to give his powerful roar and strike, when from through the flames leaps Sammiel and his forces. They take not only Onkala by surprise, but the band of attackers as well. The fighting is short-lived, as the men under Sammiel's charge take not a moment's rest and proceed with their task at hand! Foes fall like tall grass. Sammiel displays his fighting prowess and skills. During Onkala and his men's battle and folly of underestimating their foes, Sammiel and his troops waited for the perfect moment to strike. Whatever the reasoning behind the tactic, Sammiel, and the supporting forces arrive in a not-so-timely manner. But they are able to end the defending forces' attempt to fight back. Simultaneously, bodies litter the area. While the other fighters simply cease to fight and drop their weapons.

The fighting has ended. Or had it? Onkala, although injured, is not as pleased with the outcome. "Sammiel!" he shouts. "Where were you?"

"Silence, you stupid dog," responds Sammiel.

"How dare you speak to me in that manner!" insists Onkala. "You think me the fool? I had anticipated your treachery, but never would I have imagined that you would not attempt the deed yourself."

"If you believe that I would be capable of such an act, why then did you not simply have me killed in my sleep or kill me yourself?" Sammiel asks sarcastically.

"It matters not at this point," states Onkala as he takes a defensive stance. Sammiel takes notice and begins to laugh uncontrollably.

"You are truly a brave warrior, Sammiel," begins Onkala. "Even in the cradle of death, you boldly stand and laugh in its face. There is but one direction for my people and they require only one voice to lead them… and that voice is mine." And with a sharp command, Onkala orders into position men originally from his village. Most of whom arrived with Sammiel. Again, Onkala engages in one last engagement with Sammiel. "Thank you, my friend, for helping me to gain the power that my people and I needed. Now we must part ways. Send him to his ancestors to answer for his transgressions against his family and people!" Instead of the sounds of death or flesh being pierced by weapons, there is only the sound of the fires around them and the laughter of Sammiel.

"What are you fools waiting for?" insists Onkala. Again, there are the sounds of the fires and Sammiel. The reality of the situation now makes itself painfully obvious to Onkala. Continuing to make light of Onkala's plight, Sammiel approaches Onkala. All of the men immediately draw their weapons down upon Onkala. But they are halted by a simple hand gesture from Sammiel. The men retreat a few paces backwards and lower their weapons. Leaving two men facing each other. Onkala is the first to speak.

"Will you not let my own people slay me as the last insult to our ill-fated union?" asks Onkala.

"On the contrary, you filthy animal," says Sammiel. "You have served your purpose and you are correct; there is but one direction and one voice for the people. But it will not be your voice. So Onkala, as a token of my gratitude, I will slay you myself or you will slay me. Whatever you choose to believe, tonight will see the rising of one and ONLY ONE!"

The two men steady in their positions. Steely eyes focus on targets as the two begin to circle one another. Blood and sweat trickle down Onkala's forearm onto his weapon. He clasps it with both hands. He has a broken smile, feigning bravery. A rather self-pleasing smile comes across Sammiel's face. And then he charges! The sudden attack somehow startles Onkala, as he just narrowly escapes a powerful strike that mistakenly splits one of the men in half. This does not deter Sammiel from continuing his attack. Onkala can only deflect the multiple strikes as his previous wounds hinder his abilities. But they matter not to Sammiel, who presses the attack. Onkala halts an above-head strike only to find Sammiel's large and imposing foot against his chest, sending him to the ground. His roll out of harm's way is mere inches from him becoming another victim of Sammiel's mighty blade. Although the blade did no damage, the power of Sammiel's kick has caused Onkala to cough and expel blood.

Before he can recover from the impact… there is silence. Onkala looks about and sees the faces of the men surrounding him. But he does not find Sammiel. But he does notice a glimmer from the flames just beneath him. As he looks down, he can see the length of a blade dripping with blood — his blood. As he gasps for every breath, he tries to turn to see his assassin. But that will not come to pass, for just as he does so, heavy hands clap around his head and… with a mighty twist, he is dead. Sammiel is not satisfied with just defeating Onkala, no, he wants to send a message to all. Before Onkala's lifeless body touches the ground, Sammiel has hold of both of his limp arms and places his foot on his back. With a terrifying roar, Sammiel pulls both limbs from Onkala's body. Taking it further into madness, Sammiel lifts one of the limbs and drinks of its trickling blood. It is no surprise to see the horror and fear of all who witness this dastardly deed. Yet no one challenges Sammiel when, with blood oozing from his mouth, orders them to take everything and everyone that remained.

The commands are followed without question. The endeavor takes a total of four days to completely ransack the conquered village. Another full day to gather travel supplies. And finally, the expedition home begins. Not a whisper is heard nor dared uttered throughout the envoy. But the landscape is thick with dread, as all now know that the dawn of terror is born within their new and solo king. King Sammiel is supreme ruler throughout the land. His name spreads terror throughout. Majestic wildlife run in fear of the sight of Sammiel. It is as though they can sense the evil that resides within him. He is now the ultimate predator.

It has been three weeks since the journey back to Sammiel's encampment began. The sheer number of captives and the rich bounty from the spoils of his conquest have lessened the speed of the warring party, but there is nothing to fear. The victorious Sammiel and his war party have no one to oppose them! They now have traveled over open territory with no worries. Finally, their journey has reached its end. They are home. They are greeted with cheers and tears for their victory and for those who fell in battle. Alinafe, the first and most revered wife of Onkala, speaks out. "Where is my husband Onkala?" she asks without shedding a tear. No one answers. She is shrewd, so her words are carefully chosen. It would seem that the old lion has finally come to his end. With the obvious staring her in the face, she takes her leave and blends quietly into the crowd. Sammiel gives little notice to the widow and so he proceeds on.

A celebration proceeds and time moves forward. Day-to-day life continues, and Sammiel further terrorizes the lands. He and his men constantly raid other villages and take the lands. He expands his reach beyond the eye and, in doing so, he expands his terror. All people of every nation tremble in fear that he will someday be on their horizon. The number of people taken as slaves is staggering but lucrative. Sammiel has opened trade routes and slave trading along the southern coast. He has built a scheduled timeline for the grand spectacle, which he takes great pride in making an auspicious entry. His vanity knows no boundaries. He is accompanied by over two hundred men for this pompous affair. There is no regard for the lives that will and have been forever destroyed by these acts. He cares not for whom he deals with nor cares for their intentions with the people of his own homelands. Sammiel sees these actions as another portion of his imagined slight by his family and believes that he is entitled to everything or person of the land. He chose the location for his very lucrative human trading very carefully. It is surrounded by cliffs too high to attack from, with only one descending path to a vast and secluded beach that is backed only by the ocean from the rear and both sides. The waters are treacherous and can only be reached by smaller vessels that carry the human cargo back to large ships anchored just off the coast in deeper waters. It is here that his old acquaintance reemerges.

"Ahoy there, Sammiel!" a familiar voice shouts. Upon closer inspection, it is the old grizzled sea captain!

He has regained his status and managed to acquire a vessel and crew. He is attempting to regain entry into the slave trade, and what better way than to return to his most gracious supplier?

But Sammiel has no interest in the old captain these days. He has new partners and there is no shortage of options. He acknowledges the old captain in his distinctive and dismissive manner. But the captain is not one to allow himself to be denied. He takes a very unwise step towards Sammiel only to find himself to be forcibly detained by Sammiel's henchmen, as he shouts, "I have news of your family, O' great and powerful Sammiel!" This commands Sammiel's attention. With a wave of his hand, the wretched captain is released and beckoned forward. A short distance along the beach front, Sammiel's party marches forward toward very lavish quarters. In the center of the cluster of structures is a larger, more garish standout structure. It is not long before what is obvious is confirmed. Sammiel enters after his guardsmen. Light rushes from inside, illuminating the cliff side, beach, and a portion of the sea. As night begins to lay her canvas across the skies as she always does, but there is a difference this evening: night bares her anger. She brings the lightning and the roar of ten thousand drums in the thunder. And with a slow trickle as that of the small stream, the rain begins. Then the deluge begins, and it is unwavering.

Inside, illuminated by a great pit of fire in the center of the structure. Sammiel sits in the midst of a multitude of support from his foot soldiers. "Speak on this matter that you proclaim, wretched oaf," says Sammiel to the old captain. The captain is thrust to the ground at the feet of the powerful dictator. He surveys his predicament. He witnesses warriors in all areas of the structure, and all of them fiercely armed with their attention focused upon him. His apprehension is only compounded by the thunderous command, "Everyone leave me with my friend!" that bellowed from the direction of Sammiel. Stammering to find his words, the captain begins to tell of his encounter, but is abruptly commanded to cease.

Immediately the room is cleared of all save for Sammiel and the terrified huddled captain. The light from the fire in the center of the room takes on a different significance now. It gives way to two remaining figures. Once confident of their privacy, Sammiel rises and makes his way towards a table that is overflowing with lavish food and drink, all of which are for the sole consumption of Sammiel. But on this occasion, he serves himself, or so it would seem. Taking an ornately adorned goblet in hand, Sammiel pours a serving of a highly revered ale. This ale is only reserved for royalty or, in this instance, Sammiel. But Sammiel does not drink. Instead, he hesitates. With his back to the captain, he asks one question. "Tell me… are my brother and his family alive or not?" Clamoring for answers, the old captain is at a loss for words.

With a slow whirl and a friendly and inviting smile. Sammiel begins to speak with his audience of one. "Come now, my friend. Take a moment to gather yourself," says Sammiel with a tone of reassurance. In the same moment, Sammiel hands his royal chalice to the obviously agitated man. With astonishment and trembling hands, the old captain takes the chalice and, without a breath, swallows the entire contents. Smiling once more, Sammiel accepts the goblet and ushers the man to have another. Once refilled as he is just handing the goblet to the now more at ease old sea captain, Sammiel once again asks him to begin his tale.

With confidence, the captain recalls the chance encounter. And with each word, Sammiel grows more intent. He is mesmerized by the captain's words and draws ever so closely as if to hear more clearly. As the captain outlines the details of his meeting with Numair and the others, he is drinking the delicious ale and oblivious to the approaching Sammiel. He tells of uncanny abilities of the youth and of how he was thwarted in his attempt to complete his previously paid task. As he finishes his astonishing tale, he emphasizes the sighting of the band of survivors leading back to their homeland!

Just as he finishes his last gulp of the royal ale, his chalice is lowered only to find that the last sight that he witnesses are two daggers being thrust into his eyes. Sammiel had retrieved two daggers from his back hilt and thrust with a great anger into the skull of the old captain. With a scream of agony, the old captain is quickly grasped by Sammiel by the mouth and back. Lowering him to the ground, the captain hears these final words. "You have failed to complete your assignment for which you were handsomely paid. Your incompetence leaves me no other recourse for your thievery. You have gravely changed my course of action and endangered my plans!" angrily states Sammiel. It takes but a few moments for the guards to react to the blood-curdling screams of the dying man. And a wave of a hand for Sammiel to command their departure. With the taking of his last breath, Sammiel drops the dead man's body with no regard to the earth beneath him. Trembling with anger, Sammiel takes a moment to gather his thoughts and composure before exiting his quarters.

Upon his entrance into the encampment, he orders that his quarters be rid of the dead body that defiles it. Among the men that follow him, the whispers circulate with a fervor. Taking quick stock of the situation, Sammiel commands that "From this day forth, if anyone should be so brazen to attempt to bring lies to me, immediate death shall be the punishment!" A low rumble is heard from among the troops, but understood that Sammiel's words were not to be contested or questioned.

As the men proceed to remove the dead body from the confines of their commander's quarters, Sammiel slowly strolls towards the sea. Staring off through the storm into the horizon, his focus is steely and his thoughts begin to take shape. He ignores the storm and takes himself into a semi-trance like state. He calls upon his mother's spirit for guidance. Immediately, he is before her! Manyara's wailing screams demand answers.

"Sammiel! How could you fail such a simple task as to kill a few small children and old women?" she demands. Before an answer can be given, Manyara gives Sammiel his obvious course of action. "You shall maintain your composure and continue on your quest to command and rule all of the lands! Now gather yourself and prepare for that which is to come!" howls Manyara.

"Fret not, for I shall lay waste to these remnants of a time long past!" she continues. And like the puff of smoke blown away by the storm, she is gone. Sammiel finds himself once again at the edge of the encampment, staring off into the abyss. His gaze is fixed. It is said by those who witnessed this sight that it seemed as though Sammiel were actually staring into someone's face as though that person stood right in front of Sammiel…

Off in a distant part of the land to the west, another figure holds position high among trees. Prince Numair keeps a vigilant watch as his people take refuge for the night after the arduous journey of the last few days. The land in which he and his people now occupy is littered with patches of small oases. A fact best enjoyed now, for the lands ahead are not so giving. The night is filled with stars and a bright full moon. Great distances have been traveled by the prince and his people. Onward, ever dreaming of returning to a home that all embrace is different from what they were robbed of, yet they burn with desire to reclaim their homeland. The prince has chosen a well defensible location. It is lush and has a flowing stream within. The Makobo trees provide not only excellent cover, but additional food as well. The area has abundant fresh game for the group. The smaller trees and bushes form a natural boundary with the soft loam from the water's edge providing a soft night's place for the purposed people to lay for the night.

The young king is the single figure outlined by the night sky.

"I feel the presence of evil this night," he professes to himself.

"That would be your senses recognizing threats to you," his father states. "I am very proud of you, my son, but I will not keep hidden the fact that you are heading for your greatest challenge," he continues. "My brother Sammiel is aided by his mother, Manyara, who has become a servant of the darkness. Together, they will cause your journey to take our people home even more perilous. As your senses heighten, you must be ever cognizant of your every motion. Every blade of grass, every stone, every breeze that comes your way is a potential threat to you and the others, my son," his father tells him.

He is once again alone. Numair feels his muscles tensing as they bulge. His vision is keen and enhanced as he surveys the lands. He has his purpose and responsibility well embedded in his heart! His blood burns with anticipation. Numair is high in the trees to gain advantage over any that would dare to impede their rest. He takes a moment to spy down upon the people in his care as they rest weary bodies. The young king is concerned for each of them. For they cannot fathom the dangers of the journey before them. But as their chosen protector, he vows to defend them and to ensure that they are returned to the home of their forefathers! But that goes without saying. Back to the duties at hand.

Again, King Numair is the lone figure in a calm night. Focused and vigilant, the young Prince resumes his guard as he settles back among the lush branches, high among the Makobo trees. He views everything around him in a strange hue of yellow, but he cannot see darkness. A benefit that he cares not to share with others just yet. He shall rest for a short time at first light.

As the night continues and all settle down from the day, his senses tingle as though they are being watched from the very sky above. But it matters not. Uncle, I come for you… and know this, there is not enough preparation to stop my wrath, contemplates Numair as he stares into the star-filled night!

CHAPTER 9

To Walk With Strangers

The night air has a stench that is unfamiliar. But Numair's keen senses are detecting something peculiar in the air. The years of captivity have allowed young Numair to hone his skills and abilities. He is now a large, powerful young man with a regal calmness in his mannerisms. His heightened awareness has his entire body tingling. Without disturbing a single leaf, Numair descends from his perch and silently circles around to the strength of the odor. Keen vision affords the young warrior the advantage of stalking his prey, so to speak. For it is not malice in his intent, but rather curiosity. In the tall brush that surrounds the encampment, Numair holds his position and utilizes his vision and hearing. He immediately hears every blade of grass breaking from steps; he can see the smallest of branches flay back and forth from trespassers. With this knowledge, Numair begins to visually track who or whatever it is that has invaded the group's peaceful seclusion. Initially, the power to see the world as the big cat does gave the young king a fright. Over time, Numair has come to embrace the power of sight as well as many other talents that he now possessed.

Motionless, Numair slowly and carefully surveys the landscape. He listens for heartbeats, breaths, the crackle of a leaf, or the movement of the very air that surrounds the area. There! Their numbers are small. Only four bodies. Their movement is slow and stealthy, but deliberate. Strange, but their bodies are muscular and powerful. They are tall in stature, but seemingly lacking in treacherous motives or actions. They give off a new scent that Numair has come to recognize as "fear". Odd, but Numair senses that the party is more afraid to actually encounter the royal party than the off chance of facing a wild beast. The unknown party does have weapons, but they are very odd in nature. A strange, shiny metal makes up these flimsy items. They seem to be more tools than weapons. Curious.

For a short time, Numair simply observes their movements. In truth, they are not hunters or warriors, he concludes. Their movements are clumsy and lack wilderness experience of that of a seasoned warrior. It is deemed that these curious beings pose no immediate threat to the family. It was at that moment that Numair decided to make himself known to these clumsy people. But he prefers to halt them a good distance from his travel companions, so as not to disturb their much-needed slumber. So, he slowly makes his way in front of the strangers and takes to the treetops. His climb is remarkable in its speed and agility. But it is the silence of his movements that is most remarkable. Numair leaves little to no foot marks or disrupted leaves from either the branches of nearby bushes or blades of grass. Numair is aware of the moon's bright glow and takes position along an intersection of branches that allows him to hold steadfast behind the bold trunk of the tree. He listens and gauges the distance of the strangers and awaits their ideal position before introductions are made. His wait is not long, for the strangers soon make their way directly into the path in which Numair had chosen. At a perfectly timed descent, Numair leaps to the ground in front of the strangers with as much noise as a falling leaf.

Stunned, the now beset upon strangers are paralyzed in fear. Their expressions betray them as before they can run off in the other direction, Numair has leaped over them and again stands in their path of escape. They instantly relinquish their weapons and fall to their knees in utter fear. It is that very gesture that gives cause to Numair to remove his mask. Revealing a youthful, yet smiling, human face. In the moonlight, his features shown very clearly, which was a relief of sorts to the still cowering party of strangers.

Initially, Numair makes an attempt to converse with the strangers, but they are locked in fear of Numair. He resorts to gestures. His first was an extended hand to help one of the party's members to his feet. He proceeds with a simple act of friendship by offering his water gourd, as the entire party now makes their way to their feet.

For a time, there is nothing but whispers among the strangers, but that soon gives way to curiosity for the gangly men. Numair is patient as well as kind to their touching of his person and stares of wonderment. Most would not take too kindly to this behavior. Throughout all of the horror and pain that the young king has endured over the years, Numair has remained a kind spirit and has never wavered from understanding the plight of others. Over the past long months of trekking across unknown lands, Numair has grown to become a fierce and righteous king. As all become acquainted with Numair, he decides to take these people to the safety and comfort of camp. Not indifferent to the stranger's current state of mind, Numair gestures for the party to follow him.

The trek is short through the dense foliage. The group follows, but they cannot dismiss the fact that the king's movements are silent and do not disturb the jungle canvas. It serves to give further support for them to follow instructions, for the moment. Upon arrival to the encampment, Numair need not make an effort to wake his travel companions, for they are well awake and engaged in battle! All members of the king's party are ferocious in their attacks. The unknown assailants are no match. With each attacker, the outcome is the same. One man raises his weapon above his head and gives a battle scream as he rushes toward Queen Akilah. Although the years have clearly become apparent upon her physical being, she is unwavering in her focus. She tightens her grip on her spear and does a truly masterful twirl of the spear. In one motion that can only be described as awe-inspiring, she sprints deliberately towards her opponent and plants the spear tip into the ground and simultaneously launches into a flip while still maintaining her grip on the spear. As she lands, her battle stance is solid and firm. Just as quickly, she unearths the spear tip and lunges it into the throat of her attacker! All he can muster is a gurgled sound as his mouth fills with blood. With a strong kick, she dislodges her spear from his dying body! His heavy lifeless body can do nothing but collapse backward toward the unyielding soil which will now be his life departure location.

Princess Adero is not one to be overlooked. She engages with two assailants. Her combat skills reveal Kang's influence as well. The princess finds herself between two massive bloodthirsty assassins but with a flirtatious smile, she launches a lightning-fast dual dagger counter-attack. As both men initiate their advance with heavy and broad-bladed weapons, the princess swiftly strikes a Jéndŏwe (crane) pose. And just as impressive as the queen, Princess Adero begins her impressive display of combat arts. Just as the two behemoths think that they've reached their target… the princess immediately and with blinding speed glides to the ground as her legs are spread to unimaginable lengths, her toes are pointed towards the evening stars. The attackers strike the air as their strikes do not find the princess, but instead, both ill-fated men are soon experiencing searing and agonizing pain. As the princess dislodges her daggers from her attacker's groins. The princess' moves are so swift that it gives the impression that she was never engaged in the battle. As the men look in horror, blood sprays the area and coats the ground, their legs, and anyone in the immediate area! Two massive bodies fall to their knees and slowly fall forward, faces encounter the ground with a thud. Death is their outcome, but the princess has long disengaged this confrontation and moved on to another skirmish. And such are the mindsets of every member of the king's party.

For some, this may have seemed as though these moments were an eternity. But in reality, this battle was brief. The attackers numbered around twenty. As many of them fall in battle, Numair seizes the opportunity to disarm and disable one of the men. The king engages an attacker by holding his ground with no signs of fear or hesitation. As the overhead strike comes towards the king, the arm of the attacker is met with a vice-like grip. With his left hand, Numair squeezes and breaks the man's arm. With his right arm, the king takes a hold of the man's throat and lifts him from the ground effortlessly. Through the many years in exile, the once young prince, now king, has accepted and become masterful in honing his incredible powers. One would think that death will now take another traveler tonight. But that is not what transpires; instead, the king tightens his grip evenly and targeted until the man collapses into unconsciousness. All other attackers lie lifeless on the ground. King Numair's new acquaintances no longer hold apprehensions. As Numair's group assembles around the king, the new travel companions open up and begin to cheer the success of Numair and his people.

Numair instructs that his incapacitated attacker be bound. "Numair!" gleefully shouts the princess Adero! "We were all so worried that these men had dispatched you! Who are they? What happened to you?"

Numair embraces his mother and grandmother and showers them with kisses of reassurance. "I was drawn away by my new companions that accompany me," he states. It is at that moment that one of the men from Numair's reconnaissance now speaks. "Thank you, my friends," states the new friend. "My name is Bongani. We are the Sanns people. We apologize that our previous actions may have caused you due concern. We were not sure of your alliances. We presumed you to be members of these animals which you have bested in battle. They have pursued our people for some time now." Numair interrupts the enthusiastic Bongani. "A moment friend," Numair asks. "Mother, is everyone well?" Adero confidently responds with a resounding yes! She continues by stating that the men of Kang's training performed exceptionally well. "I think that I have found a new name for what I would recommend now be your new 'Royal Guards'… the 'Menokang Guard!'"

Despite the horrifying climate, the princess' bright, beautiful smile gives many reasons to rejoice. "Then let it be so," exclaims King Numair! Cheers roar through the night. But the young king has not lost sight of this evening's events. With a commanding voice, he instructs everyone to gather their belongings and prepare for departure from this place. As many do so, Numair turns his attention to his captive. The king takes the man by his bindings and drags him near the fire. The warrior, now revived from his unplanned slumber, stares at his captors, surveying the people who have now encircled his location. But Numair is studying his captive. He has specific intentions for his line of questions. He positions himself in a squatted pose, just in front of the man. In a very calm and patient manner, the king simply asks of the man, "Where is Sammiel?" Gasps are heard throughout from those in attendance.

"What nonsense is this you speak of, Numair?" asks Queen Akilah. "Grandmother, this man bears the markings of our home!" With that, Numair grasps the man's head and turns his head to reveal tribal markings familiar to the disenfranchised people. Two waving lines connecting to one vertical line placed over a circle. The mark that every member of Numair's people. But Numair senses that all is not as it seems. He proceeds to inform and identify that although the captive may bear the marks of their people, he is indeed not of them! He proceeds to point out the skin complexion of this man. "He is of a darker nature than our people," begins Numair. "His facial features have mutilations, something that we do not practice." With the revelations, the warrior smiles an eerie smile and spits on the ground towards the feet of Numair. As Numair stares at the insulting puddle of disrespect at his feet, Bongani lunges forward and attempts to slit the throat of the warrior! But he is halted in his attempt by the unyielding grasp of king Numair.

"My friend, please explain your actions," asks Numair. Bongani proceeds with a tale of terror and dogged pursuit. "Our people are nomads, we are the Khoe-sans. We are a peaceful lot that agitates not the peace or lands of others. We migrate from region to region along routes established centuries past. We are descended from the Saans and blended with the Samburu people. The knowledge gained from our ancestors, passed down through the ages and practiced to this day, has gained notoriety in many regions. Our queen, Queen Aminatu, our fearless warrior leader, is the conquest that these lowly demons seek to covet. They initially made contact under the guise of a peaceful trade. Upon being introduced to our queen, their demands were revealed. The emissary for their commander issued her the ultimatum of her hand in marriage or the death of her people. But she was greatly underestimated! Queen Aminatu responded in kind with her own terms. 'Leave our lands now or suffer my wrath,' were her terms. She proceeded to ensure that her words would not be taken lightly and executed all but three of the false emissary's party to carry back her response to their villainous commander."

"That was two moon cycles ago," (two months). "Since that time, we have been attacked on numerous occasions and with each attack the queen has demonstrated her uncanny battle skills and abilities. But the attacks have been unrelenting and have taken heavy tolls on our people. This has forced the queen to constantly move our people along known regions that only our people know. That is the cause for our being here when Numair surprised us."

"King Numair!" insists Queen Akilah. "You all are in the presence of the king of the BaFokeng people."

"You and your people are the cause of this bloodbath that has cursed the lands?" An agitated Bongani interrupts.

Queen Akilah quickly and sternly halts Bongani's accusations. "How dare you? Although I can understand your apprehensions. Please do not callously believe that we are in any fashion, are to be presumed to be a part of this butchery! We are members of the betrayed royal family of BaFokeng. My son Sammiel betrayed not only our family but all of our people as well! The quest that we partake of is of the most vital importance. We most certainly are not party to these atrocities!" "Apologies," stammers Bongani. "We are unfamiliar with everyone's status among your people. It is not my intention to offend."

"If I may proceed." With an approving nod from Numair, Bongani continues. "Our purpose here is that we were tracking signs of stalkers. We came upon your party a mere few days ago and began to watch and ensure that you were not an advance party spying upon us. Tonight's feats undoubtedly prove those impressions misguided. Now that you have revealed who you are, we most certainly must beg of you to please meet with our queen. I am certain that you will find this helpful in your quest."

Princess Adero enters into the conversation with a comforting hand upon the shoulders of Bongani. "New friends, let me assure you of no ill will towards you or your people. There is no need for apologies as, as you stated, you had no manner of knowing who we were or what our intentions would be. Come, let us all take a brief moment to council on your proposal. I am sure that King Numair would like to hear more of what you speak of, as would we all."

And with that, as the others prepare for departure, the king is joined by the queen, princess, a few trusted tribesmen as does Bongani and a few of his men around the dying flames of the fire that once burned in the night and provided comfort. All are aware of the need for expedience in leaving this location, but also the need for all to come to an agreement to venture forth together. As the group begins their conversations, Princess Adero notices that King Numair has not chosen to speak to the group. She does not inquire, for she has learned through the years since the child prince first inherited his powers, to allow him his solace. For she and every member of the family and tribe now understand that the young king is most undoubtedly in council with his elders. Initially, many found it somewhat uncomfortable to be witness to. But as time passed, so did the people's confidence in their king's abilities. For as time marched on, so did Numair's mastery of his gifted powers.

Indeed, Numair is in conference with his ancestors. "Father, it is suggested that I sway from course to place my trust upon someone whom I have no knowledge of. We have traveled nearly a year, torn away from our homelands for more than a decade and now a mere twenty or more days away from reaching our beloved lands. Our people are anxious to return to the land of our forefathers, yet I sense that it will not be easy," states Numair. A powerful voice responds. "Numair, you are wise in your assessment, my son," replies his father Girma. "I will not shield the truth from you, my son," he continues. "In less than a full cycle of the moon, you will face a great evil... your uncle Sammiel

"In less than a full cycle of the moon, you will face a great evil... your uncle Sammiel!"

"I am prepared, father," Numair replies confidently yet displaying great humility. "I have trained for this moment for years."

It is then that they are interrupted by another, yet never before heard, voice. "Prepared you have, my child," the voice interjects.

Of course, Numair, who has come to maintain control of his emotions and guards against displaying his thoughts through his expressions, is undoubtedly curious as to whom this new voice belongs.

"I am the first," says the voice. "And I have many proud moments that this family has given me by their exploits and honor. But none, my young one, has given me greater joy and hope than you, King Numair. For I am King Lobengula," the voice announces.

And indeed, among the many ancestors along the astral plains, comes forth an enormous panther! One like none of the ancestors he has ever seen.

"Numair, dumela rra, o tsogile jang," (loosely translated: Numair, hello sir, how are you), greets King Lobengula.

"Ke tsogile sentle, wena o tsogile jang" (I am fine, how are you) replies Numair.

With that response, King Lobengula unleashes a thunderous laugh and says, "It is a joy to know that you have not forgotten the language of your people. My Numair, you have proven yourself to be the best of us all," continues King Lobengula.

"Thank you, great ancestor," humbly replies Numair. "I am honored to be in your presence, O great king," he continues.

After the heartfelt pleasantries and gleeful reunion, the conversation turns to more sober and serious words of council. And what would seem to have been a lengthy time, in real time was only mere twinkling moments. With that, Numair joins the hastily assembled council as though he never left. Without hesitation, the king announces his decision to accompany their new friends. To the new friends, this seemed rather sudden. But to Numair's people, it was routine. It was at that very moment that the two most important people in the king's life approached and gave him the most loving embrace of approval before embarking upon their new journey.

CHAPTER 10

THE QUEEN OF HEARTS

A beautiful orange-tinted morning sun peeks over the horizon, gently kissing its vast garden. Flowers gracefully blossom to receive the warm sunrays full of nourishment. Blades of grass begin to salute the coming of the day as the sunshine spreads out among the plains. As the sun peers down upon the land, it can see a rather good-sized group of what resembles ants. But a closer look reveals those ants to be King Numair, his people, and their travel companions. Through the canopy of trees, a long winding trail of travelers is making their way towards unknown people and unknown opportunities or peril. Although these thoughts, feelings, or apprehensions abound, they deter not the traveling party.

"Bongani?" Princess Adero interrupts the morning's tranquil beauty. "Tell us please, where have your people taken refuge during this onslaught from the foreigners?"

With a prideful smile, Bongani replies, "We have many places that are untouched by outsiders and people of those very same lands. From the start of this terror, Queen Aminatu has divided our people into two factions. One group comprises the non-warriors, children, elderly, and the ill. They are supported by a garrison of warriors. Their location is far north to the ancient cities that were left vacant centuries ago at the basin of Mount Nyiragongo. The second faction is led by the queen herself. Our warriors number in the thousands. We are known throughout the regions for our physical prowess. Their march is ever-changing locations, but they routinely return to Mount Nyiragongo to rest and ensure the safety of the others."

"Please believe that I intend no offense, Bongani," begins King Numair. "But I must confess that I did not witness said warrior skills during our initial encounter. So, it leaves me to believe that you and your group are not privy to the warrior class of your kinsmen?"

"Not only are you a superb warrior, King Numair, but observant as well," replies Bongani. He continues by explaining that he and his men are herdsmen from the tribe. "During these tumultuous and dangerous times, all must do what must be done to aid in the success and survival of our people. Our queen could not part with any of our battle-tested warriors. One of the last and most bloody skirmishes, we spotted an advance party scouting the area. It was decided that we were to follow them and, if possible, dispatch them before they could either discover our most recent location or return to their master."

"I understand," responds Numair stoically.

"May I ask a question of you, King Numair?" asks Bongani.

"My dear Bongani, I gave no hesitation to your invitation to accompany, because it presents an opportunity for your people and your queen as well as myself and our people," replies Numair in anticipation of Bongani's question.

Princess Adero lightly laughs as she finds humor in Bongani's facial expression. For he is taken by surprise by King Numair's perception. But before he can inquire as to how the king knew what he would be asked, Princess Adero provides an explanation to their new acquaintances.

"Our king is the descendant of a long line of noble kings. There was one from that line of great kings, which earned the blessings of the great celestial beings. It was prophesied that a child born of the Lobengula bloodline would have a gift of great power bestowed upon them and their children's children. That chosen one is our king that stands before you now. King Numair," she concludes.

With the tender admiration of a loving mother, Princess Adero places her approving hand upon King Numair's shoulder. Numair's name is shouted repeatedly by his adoring and trusting people. For they and only they fully understand the extent of what the bestowing of the "Blessing" means for their people. Bongani and his people continue their march in total awe of the pride of these people. Although their numbers are mediocre, around three to four thousand or so, they are strong in their convictions. And if all are as skilled as the few that they have borne witness to, then they present themselves to be formidable opponents.

Bongani informs King Numair that their journey is roughly a ten days' march to the basin of Mount Nyiragongo. "We shall arrive in eight days, for we must make haste. Terror and bloodshed are coming, and none shall be left in its wake if we dawdle in our efforts to reach your queen in a timely manner." With confirmation from the leadership of the caravan of people, they march on.

The band of strangers, now friends, relentlessly travel day and night expeditiously. Resting in short intervals just long enough to regain strength and nourish weary souls. The less physically endowed ride the oxen-driven wagons that carry supplies and the weary. They travel over vast plains, maintaining an ever-vigilant eye for any signs of danger. Beautiful lands are viewed for the first time that harbor some of the most exotic herds of animals. Witnessing the all too well-known laws of the animal kingdom. Survival of the fittest. For death on the open plains is a way of life in the animal kingdom as Gazelles, Water Buffalo, Zebras, Warthogs, etc. are seen being stalked and taken down for the sake of feeding young and nourishment. A harsh reminder that blood should only be shed out of necessity. A methodology that Numair practiced as he and a few of his newly christened royal guardsmen, the Menokang. Every other night, the king and his men branch out from the caravan to hunt. And hunt the king does! His Menokang are astonished by his stealth and speed. Numair calls upon his panther skills to track and slay hordes of fresh game. Enough to feed the entire caravan.

As the hunt takes place, Queen Akilah and Princess Adero, along with several women and a band of Menokang guardsmen, set out to gather fresh water, grains, and vegetables as well as newly discovered herbs and roots. Again, more than enough to feed and care for the large caravan. Everyone works in unison for the sake of all. But Numair's people also gather and record information found in this previously unexplored region of the country. It is something that they have become accustomed to since their rescue.

It is the eve of the fifth day of constant trekking for the weary travelers, and Numair makes the decision to give everyone an extended night's rest. He chooses a location that offers a water source with a crescent-shaped row of tall trees to slow the harsh night winds. It serves as a shelter and defense for the exhausted travelers. The low grass is soft and pliable, this makes for a comfortable night's sleep. As many settle down for a much-earned rest from their arduous journey, numerous fire pits can be seen strewn throughout the encampment. The royal family takes time to gather themselves and take stock of all that has transpired and how they will and should proceed.

"Numair, my son," begins Princess Adero. "You seem troubled, is there something wrong?"

Numair shares his thoughts with his two most trusted and loved councils. "Mother," he replies. We've conquered countless challenges to be here now. I fear that although we are so very near to the end of our quest, there are many more perilous and dark times that lie ahead before we find peace and these horrible times are over," he confides.

Both women smile. Queen Akilah draws the group's attention to the beautiful night skies. "My dear children, look at these marvelous blessings that we have been given." All eyes gaze to the heavens. The night skies are all aglow with billions of glittering stars and cosmic bodies. At that very moment, a shower of what appears to be a formation of stars streaks across the awe-inspiring canvas. That is followed by a brilliantly white-flamed falling star, which blazes a trail down to earth toward the direction of Mount Nyiragongo. The spectacle is truly amazing. The exhibition is only interrupted by the crackling of burning logs in the warming fire pit.

Queen Akilah takes this time to advise her grandson. "Behold my king," she begins. "Just as our night presents us with these wonderful paintings in motion, so too will our destinies, although there is a predetermined path that we all have. We must be aware of the unknown that alters our course from time to time. Like the stars above, this is an inevitable fact of life. But like the stars, we all must strive to maintain our path and make our positive contributions to all mankind and mother earth." She says this as her eyes sparkle and she takes Numair's and Princess Adero's hands into her own as she gently embraces them.

"My king, you have given our people great joy. They believe and trust that you will return the people to our rightful home. But none more so than your mother and myself. We love you! Whatever path destiny holds before you, we are confident in your leadership and in what decisions you make. We support you. It has been your wisdom and guidance for ten long years that allowed the people to survive and now we all can take joy that you have brought us home, together. Now you have decided to detour, we have no doubt that you have a very important purpose. And without question, we follow."

As Queen Akilah looks at both of the loves in her life, a loud crackle from the fire causes the burning wood to heighten its glow as it breaks in two and falls among the blazing embers. That gives cause for Princess Adero to address her son. "Numair, I know, we all know that you have been in council with your ancestors." Numair, although he always suspected, was never for sure. But the expression upon his face inspires his mother to continue. "Yes, we have been aware of your visits with the ancestors for many years. And as you were becoming more powerful and skilled with your new abilities, the ancients made themselves known to your grandmother and myself!"

Numair is astonished by her words. His first reaction was to immediately rise from his seat. But the grips of his mother and grandmother restrain that action. He stammers for words, but cannot at the moment. But his eyes say all that he intends. As Princess Adero continues, she informs her son that although they received moments in time with the ancestors, their time was limited to just a few occasions. Queen Akilah gives confirmation of what her daughter-in-law says. She goes on to tell the young king that she knows of the purpose he has been sent to this region. And that she understands that his choice to follow his path was not an easy decision. And that she knows that it weighs heavily upon him. But she also tells him, "You have not been led astray by your ancestors. Trust once again in their wisdom. Use all that you have learned and experienced to the fullest. For soon, you will have completed all that is required by the Great Celestials to fully receive your cherished gift. You should be vigilant as well as just when all is said and done. Above all, your destiny is truly yours. But you cannot control that of others. As king, you influence many and touch their lives with every decision that you make. But not all will want what you have forged for the greater good of all. Know this, my son. Your destiny has been marred by heartache, pain, and strife. You have grown to be a wise and powerful king. There is no other more suited to accomplish this task."

With that being said, the trio enjoy a long and loving embrace. They continue their conversation for a short time more before retiring for the night. Sentries keep watchful eyes for the safety of the slumbering group. For all understand what awaits them at journey's end.

Night not only provides much-needed rest and revitalization, but bloodshed also uses the canvas of darkness. Not far away, Sammiel's forces can be found engaged in combat. Their tactics are simple, blitz and scatter the opponent, then overwhelm them with numbers. Numbers which Sammiel has amassed through years of subjugating neighboring tribes. Sammiel commands his massive force through fear of death. All have borne witness to his murderous actions. Many brandish badges of Sammiel's wrath. Horrid mutilations are the norm throughout the ranks of these warriors. They are well fed and disciplined. Deadly armed squadrons are rewarded for their victories by being allowed to live. On their return from battles, these rigid killers are given the women that they capture for pleasure. If a warrior is reported to have shown mercy in battle, once the victory has been assured, they are swiftly removed from the land of the living. If a brave warrior becomes injured in battle, he is taken back to the main encampment. There he is cared for by many medicine men and women from different factions absorbed into this massive army. It is the warrior's hope that the wound can be cared for. But for those that are deemed to have no hope for recovery, their fate is sealed. Formation is called and the wounded warrior is tied to a tall carved bare tree. This tree is one of many that accompanies the warring army on every expedition. Once bound to the tree, a commander gives honor to the warrior for his service for the great empire, then demands accolades from all present. As the masses chant, the warrior is beheaded.

These slaves are what Queen Aminatu's forces are locked in combat with. Her forces prove most formidable. They wage battle upon dry, rugged terrain. There is foliage, but it is harsh and brittle. Spiny trees decorate the landscape. The area leads to small foothills. It is no accident that Queen Aminatu has chosen this location to confront the two garrisons of Sammiel's forces, roughly one thousand men. Her fighters begin to give ground and eventually turn and run up an embankment. They are closely followed by the invaders. But that proves to be a fatal error! It was a planned tactic the queen herself orchestrated. Along the backside of the embankment, the queen's reinforcements are hidden. Their span encompassed the top of the embankment to just out of sight of the lower terrain. As her initial forces occupied Sammiel's bloodthirsty and determined henchmen, the lower section of fighters encircled them from the right and from behind. Once higher ground was obtained, the queen issued the command for her troops to strike.

The strategic move proved flawless, as Sammiel's men have never encountered prey that countered their advance with preemptive strikes. Although Sammiel's troops are clearly in a defeated position, they continue to fiercely fight on. They fight with the same ferociousness as they did at the very start of this skirmish. In the end, all lay dead or dying. Bodies littered the battlefield and foothills. Queen Aminatu's commander hastily ordered that her wounded be rounded up along with her dead. As dawn's light saunters onto the horizon, it finds only offerings to the local wildlife lying on blood-soaked soil.

It is little more than a day's march before the triumphant queen returns to her base camp with her warriors. Aminatu's commander, Zuberi, gives instructions for all to rest and tend to the wounded. But within the sixth hour, to be prepared to move the encampment to a new and safer location. Zuberi is a foreboding figure. He towers over the average man or woman.

He is battle-hardened through the years of protecting his tribe. His devotion to the preservation of his people's way of life is just a component of his rigid line of thinking. He is of the traditional belief in thinking that a woman should not be his people's Monarch. He believes that it is a man's position. Although he understands how Queen Aminatu came to be the ruler of his people, he does not approve. He was the most trusted combat advisor of the now deceased king, King Oba Sunni, Queen Aminatu's father.

Before the war, the king was mysteriously poisoned. No one was apprehended for the crime, as it was public and it was the king himself who served himself both drink and food. No others became ill nor died. Zuberi took the crime as a personal failure. For not only was he the loyal commander, but his friend as well. That gave cause for him to pledge himself to take a place beside the successor to the king, his daughter the princess, now Queen Aminatu. That is, he would remain so until a male suitor could prove himself worthy of becoming king to Queen Aminatu. Thus, that male would take the mantle of leadership and the balance would be restored in the hierarchy of Zuberi's people's way of life. All would have come to pass, but for the invasion of those who would take what does not belong to them and blatant disregard for the lives of others. The war has prevented the ritual from commencing. In that time, the queen has proven herself to be something of an enigma.

The queen possesses beauty and grace not seen before. Her skin is flawless, yet she is a warrior. She is cunning, yet demure. She shows remarkable skills in the day-to-day politics of her people. She navigates the diplomatic terrain of neighboring tribes by convincing them to join in the fight once she can join with a yet unknown ally. By volunteering her forces to combat the oncoming invaders, she convinces the tribes that if they do not come together in a united front, that divided they will perish one by one like so many others. In turn, passage and assistance are granted throughout the lands. More importantly, the people adore her bravery and courage. That is the basis for Zuberi's loyalty to his queen.

Aminatu uses these moments to decompress and bathe. Her handmaidens have drawn a bath and prepared a sumptuous meal. As she is handed a goblet of wine, she dismisses all and asks not to be disturbed. All comply with no questions. Guards post outside of her makeshift quarters at a respectful distance at both the front and the rear of the queen's chambers. The queen stands in the center of her field tent. She removes her sandals and tosses them away from her presence as if they disgusted her. Her feet relax as she wriggles her toes on the lush fur carpets that cover the entire dirt flooring in her tent. Aromatic candles fill her quarters with exotic scents as the shadows from their flickering flames dance against the tent wall. The queen removes her hardened animal skin and shiny metal armaments and weapons. She lifts her headdress and carefully places it upon a carved stand for it. Next to be removed is her undergarment, which is tossed into a basket that the handmaidens used to gather and wash the queen's clothing. Lastly, the queen, now deep in thought, removes the hair combs that ornately hold her beautiful, and curly flowing hair in place. She stands naked in the center of her field tent, alone. She stares sadly at her shadowy form against the tent walls and sighs.

Aminatu slowly enters herself into her bath. The water is warm and comforting. Lavish oils and scents fill the wooden tub with wonderful aromas and enticing fragrances. Taking a moment to take in all that has transpired, she submerges completely under her bath waters. There she remains for a brief period, then emerges and gasps for air. She clutches herself with both arms as she pulls her knees inward towards her torso. The queen is clearly using her privacy to succumb to the pressures of leadership and the horrible truths of battle. She whispers to her dead mother and father.

"Why have you been taken from me?" she asks in tears. "I am alone and I fear that I cannot be the ruler that you were, father! Mother, you left our lives many years ago, but you have never forsaken me. But it has been ages since you have come to me. And your unexpected return was very cryptic in nature. I do not understand," she says as tears stream along her face lines.

The queen's mother died in childbirth. But her spirit would often visit her daughter to guide her as she maneuvered through life's maze of obstacles that only a mother could advise a daughter. But shortly before Oba Sunni was murdered, the visits ceased. That was almost four months ago. But the night after Sammiel's emissaries met their fatal end, Queen Aminatu received an unexpected vision. In her vision, she, and what appeared to be different members from an assortment of tribes, could not move forward as they journeyed across black soil that bellowed grey smoke in intervals. The air was thick with dust and debris. Still, the queen and her companions attempted to move forward with what could only be described as a nonexistent wall or barrier. A figure rushes from her group to another location towards the barrier. That figure of a man is instantly burned to ash! This happens again and again. The queen struggles to wake from this horrific scene, but it would seem that she is forced to witness this. In the vision, Aminatu herself steps out in the forefront of the group. She raises her sword high, preparing to give the order to fully charge the barrier, she is halted by a shadowy figure emerging from the smoke and dust.

The figure is that of a man whose face she cannot see. But she seems familiar with the man. He takes her into his arms and turns to face the barrier that once impeded Queen Aminatu and the others. Together they advance as though nothing was ever there. Her vision continues. As the group moves onward, Aminatu looks down to see that they walk on carpets of blood. The air rains grey mud. All signs of life are charred to resemble the fire pits after they have been extinguished. Dark clouds have blacked out the skies. There are bodies sprawled about that are ablaze with those bodies posed in time. As they proceed through this garden of death and destruction, Aminatu is not in fear. The man in her vision has her by her hand; she feels safety. The vision is a mass of images that only serve to intensify the cryptic message that Queen Aminatu is confident is her mother giving her warning of what is to come. The journey continues with the group coming face to face with a giant horned black creature. The eyes of the creature are flames. Its muscular body towers over ten men. Queen Aminatu and all present tremble in fear, save for the faceless man. He maintains her hand in his. And he plunges his hand into the heart of the beast. All sounds disappear and then brilliant light flashes. In the end, the queen sees nothing familiar. Just graceful waterfalls flowing into a beautiful lagoon. Surrounded by awe-inspiring cliffs. Birds, butterflies, and gorgeous plant life cover the landscape. And again, without warning, she is awake.

That vision has troubled Queen Aminatu ever since. She can only trust that it came from her mother. And that she must decipher the cryptic warning soon. But she is resilient. Aminatu briskly washes her face and body to satisfaction. Once out of the bath, she dresses herself in fresh battle attire and undergarments. She calls out to the posted guards to summon Zuberi to her quarters. As she awaits his arrival, she begins to enjoy a much-needed meal. It is astonishing to witness the transformation from just a few short moments before. That is a testament to the queen's intestinal fortitude.

Upon arrival, Zuberi requests permission to enter, which is granted. Accompanying him are other advisors to the queen. But ultimately it is the queen and Zuberi that decide on how the tribe is to proceed. Queen Aminatu asks of Bongani's scouts' whereabouts. Blank stares are what she encounters until a low-level advisor, Edda, speaks up.

"They have yet to return, my queen," she says. "But that is not to say that they have met their demise either," she sheepishly utters.

"Speak up, Edda," commands Aminatu!

Edda stammers to continue, but the words are lodged in her throat. Aminatu gently addresses the woman with a warm and supportive hand of encouragement to continue. And she does.

"If they were killed, my queen, some gruesome notification would have been sent by that animal."

She is pleased by the queen's response.

"That is an excellent point and you are correct, Edda," replies the queen. "Henceforth, I do not expect a single person to have fear of input," she continues. "For as my advisors, you all were chosen because you have proven yourselves on countless occasions. Is that understood?" she commands. They finalize their council and move on to overseeing the teardown of the encampment. Edda has been given the task of releasing three Hoopoe birds. They are codes for groups sent out from the main tribe of people. One bird indicates that the tribe has not moved, two is to inform of conflict, and the third bird indicates that the tribe has traveled to a safe location that is decided upon before the parties depart the main body of the tribe. With that, the band of Nomadic people had cleared the area and left no trace of their ever being there. Mid-morning would shine down upon what appears to be an untouched-by-man portion of terrain. Animals once again felt free to roam the area, plant life stretched out to fully partake in the nourishment of the glorious sunrays. Winds howled throughout mountain passes and foothills searching, but finding no one.

CHAPTER 11

UNITED WE STAND

Twenty days prior, Sammiel meets with his generals. He is determined to take Queen Aminatu as his. "Lord Sammiel," inquires the powerful general, Imari.

"What is so unique about this one vagabond of a queen? You are the all-powerful ruler of a vast kingdom. You may have any woman of your choosing to be your bed wench."

Without warning, Sammiel hurls a mighty backhand to the general's face!

"Speak again of my queen in that manner and I will have you slaughtered," angrily commands Sammiel.

The remaining generals in attendance simply maintain focus on the carved table with a drawing upon it that they encircle. Among the generals are their lieutenants, to include Imari's son, Chidubem. A hush falls upon the room as the emasculated general takes a cloth from his waist to contain the blood that flows from his mouth. Sammiel turns his attention back to his business at hand.

"I want two attacking legions to head north, for this mountain basin," he says as he points to a crude sketch from an advance scouting party. "They will overwhelm her forces here and that will leave her vulnerable for capture. True, they are nomads, but they have bested you generals repeatedly!" he screams.

Without taking a breath, Sammiel orders a legion be sent up from the south to probe for any counterattacks or prevent any escape.

Sammiel suddenly halts his tyrannical verbal assault. Everyone looks on, expecting more to be communicated. Instead, they witness Sammiel in what could only be described as a tormented conversation with himself. But Sammiel is actually conferring with Manyara, his mother.

"You are weak," she vilely tells him. "How do you presume to be king of anything," she continues, "if you are not willing to take what you want?"

"I take what I want," he replies, but he appears more like a child justifying his stance.

"Stop muddling around like a scalded dog!" she now screams hauntingly. "Take heed, Sammiel, because you lacked the courage to kill everyone from the royal family. Your nephew is claiming to be king and many are beginning to listen to the murmurs of his existence. Because you have practiced slackness, he now makes his way towards you and possibly to the very woman that I told you to find and take as your own! Can you find the courage to do what you could not before?" she asks.

"Yes, mother," Sammiel replies.

"Can you protect that which you have fought for?"

Again, Sammiel replies with a resounding, "Yes!"

"Then how do you propose to do so if your warriors do not respect you?" she goads.

Emphatically, Sammiel shouts out, "I will show you, over and over again!"

When he is finished, Chidubem can be found at his feet on bended knees, clutching a profusely bleeding space where his ear was once attached.

The stunned assembly can only watch in horror! Sammiel calmly commands that the boy be attended to and for the generals to carry out his instructions. General Imari assists his son to his feet. As he clutches the injured Chidubem, they exit Sammiel's quarters to the disapproving eyes of the encampment. At dusk, Sammiel orders a feast of battle be prepared.

"We are at victory's threshold," he exclaims! "When our advance warriors return with our new queen, we have become unstoppable. None would dare challenge our rule. And we shall all bask in the glory of victory!"

Roars of cheers from the massive army echo throughout the land. But not all share those sentiments. Throughout the army, many share disapproving glances. Yet they are silent.

It is present day and weary travelers have arrived at their destination, greeted by cheering hordes. They traveled the remaining days at a furious pace. Venturing into unknown lands full of new wonders. Their journey took them to a majestic body of water, which was fed by a glorious waterfall. It is here that Numair and his people discover some of the means of travel by Bongani and his people. For high along the cliff pass of the waterfall lay hidden a cave. This cave served as transport to an even more sight to behold. As the travelers exited the cave, they came upon the glorious settlement of Bongani's people. Game seems abundant here in this paradise, as scores of animals can be seen from every direction. Lush trees formed a canopy that camouflaged the sprawling tribesmen ahead. With a strange vocal signal that is replied to by the like, Bongani turns and smiles to all, saying, "Come, my friends, we are home!"

The Khoe-San people chant victorious return songs for the returning tribesmen. Bongani is specifically greeted by a woman leaping into his arms and showering him with kisses of joy! Once he disengages his kiss from the woman, Bongani, still embracing the woman, introduces her.

"My friend, please let me introduce you to my wife, Lerato. She is the mother of my children and the reason for my existence," he says with a smile as wide as a hippopotamus.

She is a particularly joyous woman. She has a smile that is as bright as the sun itself. A stout woman, with a jolly welcoming face. Both are soon over-run by a bevy of children from all age groups.

"And these are my children," proudly proclaims Bongani.

Through the crowd, men make their way to Bongani and his new acquaintances. It is commander Zuberi. He clasps Bongani about his shoulders and renders a welcoming smile, not something that is often seen by the people.

"Ah, little brother, it is good to see you," he says with an obviously gladdened heart.

"And you as well, big brother," replies Bongani as he embraces his brother.

This action gives cause for Numair and the others to inquisitively glance at one another. For this is indeed unexpected. The two men are clearly the opposite of one another. Despite the spectacle and jubilant fanfare, the matter of their arrival remains to be addressed. But it is Zuberi who is vigilant in his duties.

"And just who have we here?" he asks.

Bongani is joyful to make introductions. He introduces the Queen Mother Akilah, as well as Princess Adero. He motions their attention to the mass of people from their tribe. And finally, he introduces King Numair. He urges Zuberi to hastily arrange for Queen Aminatu to meet with King Numair. He goes on to tell Zuberi that he believes that King Numair and his people can definitely aid in the war with Sammiel. He, however, withholds the fact that the two men and people are of the same kinship.

Zuberi moves to confront Numair and, although Zuberi is a fine specimen of a man, Numair towers over him. But still maintains his stern posture as he and Numair clap forearms as a form of warriors greeting one another. It also serves as a form of measuring your opposition. With that, Zuberi quickly learns of the tremendous power that Numair possesses. That gave cause for Zuberi to give slightly in facial expression. He quickly releases their clasp and gives a command for the new guests to be given food and water. He also insists that Numair and only Numair accompany him to the queen. Although this is not uncommon, Princess Adero petitions to join in meeting the queen. But Numair turns to her and the others.

"Mother, everyone, please be mindful that we are guests to strangers and their customs. Let us not insult their way of life. I will accompany commander Zuberi and all will be well."

A runner is sent to inform the queen of the incoming stranger. Numair, after ensuring that everyone is being attended to, joins Zuberi, Bongani, and a detachment of warriors to be presented to the queen.

The runner announces to Queen Aminatu that Bongani and the rest of his party have returned safely and that they have numcrous people accompanying them. He also tells of commander Zuberi's intentions of presenting the stranger king to the queen. Aminatu thanks the runner and commands that food and wine be prepared for her guests' arrival. But she also commands that the guards enter the quarters as well as maintain sentries posted just outside. The queen is cautious in her thinking and decides not to leave anything to chance.

So, she places weapons near her makeshift throne and about her person. As she awaits Zuberi's arrival, she requests that her fire pit be stoked and fed until it became a roaring fire.

Upon arrival, Zuberi enters alone. "Queen Aminatu," he begins. "Bongani and his party have returned with tales of battle and strangers that he says dispatched Sammiel's forces with ease. Bongani insists that the people would be of great importance to aid our people in this war," he concludes.

"How do you find these people, Zuberi?" asks Queen Aminatu.

"My queen, I have only just encountered the strangers," replies Zuberi. "But I find it odd that the timing of their arrival coincides with the latest attacks. I am guarded of their arrival," he concludes.

"I see," Aminatu responds. "Let us entertain these strangers. We will determine their intentions from our conversation," she says.

"If you would please, my queen," adds Zuberi. "I have ordered that only their king accompany me to meet with you."

"Then let us not keep our interesting visitor waiting," Aminatu commands.

Zuberi motions to a guard to summon Numair to enter. And as Numair enters, his head is lowered to account for the low-level entrance into Queen Aminatu's quarters. But as he rises to give himself an erect stance, he and Queen Aminatu lock glances for a moment. As Numair advances closer to the queen, it is only the swift actions of the guards' drawing weapons to signal that he is dangerously close to exceeding the boundaries, that brings the queen and Numair back to present circumstances. Blushing from her actions,

Queen Aminatu gives welcome to Numair. "Welcome, King Numair," she says.

"Thank you, Queen Aminatu," Numair replies. "I am pleased and honored that you have granted an audience."

Tossing her hair to the right side of her head, the queen smiles and returns to the business at hand. "I must ask," she begins. "Why have you come to these lands?"

Numair's reply raises the queen's curiosity. "I am no stranger to the lands south of your kingdom, dear queen," Numair proceeds to inform the queen. "I am the grandson of King Chimeratu, ruler of the southern kingdom." The room fills with muffled whispers. "Our kingdom was once a peaceful tribe," he states as he ignores the chatter about the room. "We were the end result of years of conflict between warring tribes centuries ago. It was my great ancestor, which destroyed the turmoil and carnage of that time. And united many tribes, but also allowed others to choose their own paths. All with the promise of peace. For that, our family was promised a gift to an heir of my great ancestor. As I stated before, my people resided in peace for centuries. But some fourteen years ago, a particularly vile tribe sought great power through conquests. They had ransacked many tribes before they set their sights upon my people. We would not be such willing victims of their brutality. My grandfather, father, and uncle led our warriors to victory on many occasions. But at some point, my uncle Sammiel decided to force the fates. It was his belief that if he were to destroy the royal family and destroy our village, that he and only he would be the recipient of the long before prophecy. His butchery had no boundaries or compassion.

"He betrayed our family and our people for his gain with no remorse." Somberly ending his tale, Numair simply gazes into the eyes of Queen Aminatu. She too became enchanted with a star-crossed gaze into Numair's eyes. Zuberi notices a possible attraction and quickly attempts to bring the queen's attention back to the council.

"King Numair," he judgmentally inquires. "That, my friend, is a wonderful tale, but the question remains as to why have you entered into our region?" he asks.

Numair, now the consummate diplomat, turns his gaze to Zuberi. But his gaze is not of the same tenderness. "My people and I," Numair begins, "have been invited by your brother, Bongani. Did his actions overstep his boundaries? Or has his hospitality been a sole act of kind spirit?" Before an answer can be offered, Numair continues. "Be that as it may, I have been counseled that the joint efforts of the Mighty Queen Aminatu's forces, combined with our people and a host of others, would be the pivotal pact that would turn the tide of this war."

Zuberi looks to the queen for approval, but none is offered. He himself being a wise diplomat, Zuberi adjusts his approach. "Forgive me, King Numair, for my impertinence. We only seek to uncover you and your people's purpose for gracing our lands with your presence," he sheepishly asks. "Can you please instill us with your purpose?" he bluntly inquires.

Numair smiles and addresses Zuberi. "Our purpose," begins Numair, "is simple. We seek to retake our family's lands and the throne. And I will remove the usurper from his false and illegitimate kingdom. I will return our betrayed people to their homelands and bring peace back to the many regions who have suffered at the hands of the bloodthirsty Sammiel," he answered intensely! "Our purpose here is to seek an alliance of forces to unite for that same purpose. For if each tribe of people," Numair continues, "chooses to stand alone, then destruction of that people is assured. And having experienced it firsthand, no man should ever have their freedoms or life taken from them or shackled and bound to another man's whim! That is the path that yours and any other people choose if we do not come together," he concludes.

Queen Aminatu interjects, "King Numair," she begins. "We are grateful for you and your people's arrival. We welcome you all and will feast your arrival tonight! Edda," beckons the queen.

"Yes, my queen," proudly responds Edda.

"Have food and drink prepared for our guests. And arrange for sleeping quarters for everyone please," commands Queen Aminatu as she smiles at commander Edda. "Commander Zuberi," the queen continues, "a moment, please. King Numair, please allow my warriors to escort you to your family."

"Thank you, Queen Aminatu," answers Numair. "I thank you and your people for your hospitality, we are most humbled for your generosity," says Numair as he slightly bows his head yet maintains eye contact with the queen. She, beyond her control, again smiles and runs her fingers through her hair ever so innocently.

As Numair exits, he has the scowl of Zuberi. Upon Numair's departure, Zuberi approaches the queen. "My queen," he inquires as he bows his head in respect. While remaining seated, Queen Aminatu dismisses all present save for Zuberi. Once all have cleared, she seeks Zuberi's council. "I do not wish to become taken for a fool by this man and his people," she begins. "But my father has told me of such a people many years before. But in his tales of their horrifying end, the entire royal family was murdered. What say you, commander Zuberi?" she asks.

"My queen, I too am aware of that tragedy," he responds. "But the details from time were inconclusive as to the actual outcome. But this I am sure of, my queen," he continues. "Upon the death of King Chimeratu, most of the tribesmen were murdered and the remaining reluctantly were absorbed into Sammiel's ranks. I do not know if this 'King Numair' is who he confesses himself to be or not. But I would advise caution in our dealings with this lot." Having regained her composure, Queen Aminatu takes a moment to ponder the quandary and replies, "Agreed."

"Ensure that the perimeter is patrolled and I will engage King Numair by the water's edge. You will accompany the two of us. I would like this king to allow himself to let his guard down if we are in a different setting. It is my hope to discover any untruths from our guest," she instructs.

"As you command, my queen," replies Zuberi. And he bows as he exits the queen's quarters.

Numair, returned from his visit with the queen, is besieged by questions from his mother. "Well?" she interrogates in a most inquisitive manner. "What of their queen, Numair?"

"All is to be expected, mother," Numair says, trying to put any fears or doubts to rest. "She and her people are quite naturally curious of our entry into their lands unannounced. It is rightfully so that they would give pause to allowing just any stranger entry during a time of war," he continues. "I am sure that through all that they have experienced, that they feel the need to keep a watchful eye out for any signs of danger."

"And you would be quite correct, King Numair," interjects Zuberi, as he has approached Numair and company. "You are astute, young King Numair," says Zuberi. "Queen Aminatu requests of you a private audience," he reports.

Both Queen Mother Akilah and Princess Adero glance at one another in astonishment. But it is Queen Mother Akilah that ushers the king off. "Be gone with you, my king," she says as she shoves the now shy king out with Zuberi. "One must never allow a queen to await your presence once you have been summoned," she says as she playfully jostles with Princess Adero. Both beam with smiles of pride and love. For they have not experienced Numair to show interest in any woman, as he has been so consumed with responsibility that he gave no thought to such notions.

As Numair and Zuberi venture through the encampment, many pause and give curious stares. Undoubtedly questioning the strangers' intentions, but unlike Zuberi and the queen's council, the people only whisper and wonder. Yet Numair remains regal and renders warm smiles throughout his trek through the camp. Just at the encampment's edge, Zuberi, sensing an opportunity, halts Numair with his hand braced against his chest. He turns to Numair with no qualms, tells him, "I am not privy to your true intentions, King Numair. But heed my words, if you prove yourself anything other than what you have proclaimed this day, I will have your head staked in front of my quarters for all pretenders to bear witness. And your skin shall serve as grain bags used by the elderly women." Whatever designs you have for our queen, I would advise that those thoughts vanish as the smoke from a fire," he issues these threats of harm as he flashes a rather sinister grin. Numair only half looks at the man and continues on.

Walking along a grassy path, Numair takes in all of the scenery. The quite rapidly flowing waters of the river that borders this menagerie of sights and sounds. Exotic birds fly overhead, giving the impression of an explosion of colors across the sky. It is truly a place of serenity. They walk for a short distance and come upon the queen. When they reach Aminatu, Zuberi excuses himself from their company. Graciously, Queen Aminatu grants his leave. Aminatu extends her gratitude for Numair accepting her invitation. Numair, in turn, thanks the queen for the invitation. Gratuitous behavior dispensed the two royals begin.

It is Numair who initiates the conversation. "May I ask," he begins. "Why have you chosen to engage in conversation here?"

Aminatu is coy in her response. "My dear King Numair, I felt that we could be more willing to speak freely if it were just the two of us," she says.

Numair quickly interrupts her by telling her, "Please call me Numair."

"And you may call me Aminatu." The two smile at one another. They move on with the conversation. Again, it is Numair who initiates the conversation.

"Aminatu, all that I have professed to be true, is indeed the truth," he begins. "The only information that I have not divulged is that Sammiel murdered my grandfather. And that he sold the remaining family members into slavery. He attempted to erase our very existence. And for that treachery, I seek to avenge the suffering and horror bestowed upon not only my family, but for all of our people. But now I must include all who have suffered horrific deeds done unto them at his hands. I can assure you, Aminatu, that we are on the same path."

Upon those words, Aminatu allows Numair to take her hand. He cradles them and gently closes his eyes. All the while, the queen does not halt his actions. On the contrary, she moves closer to his body, so close that she can feel his warm breath upon her face. Numair suddenly realizes his actions and quickly releases the queen's hand. He stammers to beg her forgiveness as he backs away from her. She too has come to the same conclusion and simultaneously does the same.

"Please forgive my actions, Aminatu," says Numair, clearly embarrassed. "I have never done such a thing."

"No need for forgiveness, Numair," she replies, as she beams with girlish excitement. "Have you, a king, never known a woman?" she asks.

Uncomfortable, Numair answers, "I have never known of a woman that gave me to express an interest… until now."

Aminatu raises her hand to cover her mouth as she gives a little laugh. "Apologies, Numair," she asks. But Numair, having never experienced courtship or the little nuances of romance, is flustered and seeking escape from the situation. But the beautiful Aminatu takes him by his hand into both of her hands.

"Dear Numair," she begins, "please do not be offended by my laughter. On the contrary, I laughed because we are quite the pair, you and I. For I have never known a man and honestly, I do not know the proper thing to do in the realm of courtship." With that, they both burst into laughter.

The two royals remain in conversation for hours. Exchanging tales of adventure and horror. They learn of the heart-wrenching path for both that gave rise to their current stations. They blissfully lost track of time as they found joy and kinship in one another. She is fascinated to hear of the wonders that Numair and his people were exposed to and the knowledge gained from their time within the compound of Lady Rebecca. Of Kang and his teachings and how he is now a missed member of their family. On and on the two talked at length of their reluctance to be rulers. But how they have obligations to their respective peoples. There is a long gaze into each other's eyes, which causes the pair to experience wave after wave of new emotions.

But their time is interrupted, "My queen, all await your arrival to begin the feast," loudly proclaims Zuberi. The startled couple compose themselves and join Zuberi and his guards. Zuberi allows the queen to pass, but halts Numair with a tight grip on his arm. Numair's ever-present smile is flashed upon Zuberi. But Numair has come to the conclusion that Zuberi has a lesson coming to him that is long overdue. Smiling, he takes Zuberi's hand and with the slightest pressure, he squeezes his hand, nearly crushing it. This gives cause for Zuberi to unleash a painful scream. All turn to find the cause, only to find Numair holding Zuberi aloft. His feet not touching the ground and Numair not straining.

"Now commander Zuberi," says Numair, "I have no doubt that someone of your status is well aware that one should not place one's hand upon someone of royalty. Is that not correct?" he asks.

"Yes, yes, yes," answers Zuberi as he clutches his injured hand. "Please accept my apology for my impertinence, KING NUMAIR," shouts Zuberi. This causes Aminatu to try to hide her amusement. Instead, she gives a clever observation.

"King Numair," she begins, "I believe commander is expressing his way of asking you for a demonstration of your strength," as she smiles and continues on the hike back to the village.

Numair, still smiling at commander Zuberi, politely offers Zuberi and his guards to join he and his Menokang in their morning training session if he would like to learn more. An offer that is reluctantly accepted by Zuberi.

At the feast, everyone is enjoying the celebration. And the company of strangers begins to form bonds of solidarity. Queen Mother and Princess Adero chatter like gleeful children as they watch the interactions between Aminatu and Numair. So too does Zuberi. But nevertheless, it has been long since Numair's and Aminatu's people have had anything to celebrate, so this night is especially joyous for the people of both tribes. As festivities abound, Queen Aminatu rises to her feet. That signaled a silence of the festivities. "We are pleased to welcome our new friends to our lands. Please extend to them every courtesy as though they were one of us," she concludes! Her message is met with a resounding roar of cheers from the people! Everyone joined in the celebration this night, and all fully embrace their union. That is all save for one. The celebration carries on into the late-night hours. Numair extends his gratitude as he excuses himself for the night. Queen Aminatu bids him a well night's rest, yet she harbors a sense of loss in his absence. Princess Adero does not overlook this and simply smiles.

Just before dawn, in a clearing away from slumbering villagers, a small army is hard at work. It is Numair and the Menokang. They are training in the taught lessons of Kang. Coming through the clearing is Zuberi, accompanied by a handful of guards. As they come closer, the unthinkable occurs. Zuberi and the guards burst into uncontrollable laughter. Their crude and disrespectful behavior does not deter the men from their focus. As the guards continue with their heckling, Zuberi sees that the men are disciplined and unwavering. He is determined to alter that. He callously marches right into Numair's path as he trains. But Numair only smiles, erects himself calmly and chants a strange command. Instantly, the warriors halt and erect themselves. Zuberi, although a skilled warrior, has never seen such discipline. He can only watch in amazement as Numair issues what Zuberi can only assume to be marching instructions. Because a single line of men begins a synchronized march. One by one, line by line, the process is repeated until the men have formed a square pattern. With a word from Numair, they sit, silent, motionless and focused.

It is then that Numair turns his attention to Zuberi. "Good morning, commander," he says. "I am most pleased that you have decided to join us," he concludes.

"What manner of fighting is this?" rudely asks Zuberi. "You and your men give the appearance of women dancing around the flames from last night's feast," he continues with a hardy laugh.

"Ah yes, it would give a certain opinion to the untrained," replies Numair. But as Zuberi begins to show his distaste for his statement, Numair offers a challenge. "Would commander Zuberi like to pit a skilled member of the guard say, one of my guards as demonstration?" Numair inquires.

That seems to please Zuberi. He flashes a wide smile and calls forth a single warrior's name… "CHIDIKE!" From the rear of the queen's guard appears a giant of a man. Broad of shoulders, massive arms, with the chest of rhinoceros and legs as thick as a tree trunk. Numair motions the man into the center of the formation of his men. Then he too calls a single name… "Olufemi." An excellent specimen of a man rises to his feet. He bows to Numair, then proceeds to bow to every side of the square formation. Chidike and Zuberi become agitated and urge a fight to begin. Numair simply lifts his hand as to signal patience. Olufemi walks to the center of the formation and faces Chidike. Chidike and Zuberi stare at one another in bewilderment. Unable to contain himself any longer, Zuberi pushes Chidike forward. Chidike rushes toward his opponent, screaming a battle cry and muscles bulging. Olufemi simply lowers himself into a sturdy fighting stance. Timed perfectly, Chidike is grasped by his forearms. His momentum aids in the action that occurs next. Olufemi falls backward with his right foot placed in the center of Chidike's chest. Before he comprehends what was happening, he was airborne. And before he lands on his back, Olufemi is airborne with both feet placed squarely in Chidike's chest. The impact from the ground and the force from Olufemi renders Chidike unconscious.

An outraged Zuberi launches an attack upon Numair with a broad swing of his sword. A calm Numair sidesteps and turns his body. The miscalculation causes Zuberi to go off balance and stumble to the ground. He quickly rolls and regains his attack mode. Again, he swings, but this time Numair simply claps his outstretched sword arm and rapidly strikes in two places. Numair ends his counterattack with a crushing elbow strike to the bridge of Zuberi's nose. Zuberi's only course of action is to drop his weapon and yield. Yet his pride will not allow this. He presses the attack. A futile attempt at best. Numair strikes him center of his chest with an open palm, which is followed by a strike of his wrist of the same hand to Zuberi's chin. And the match is over. Zuberi is awakened by a douse of water. He jumps up, shaking the water from himself yet still a bit dazed. He searches for and finds Numair. He stares long at the young king with a vicious scowl. Then suddenly bursts into laughter. "Well done warriors, well done," says Zuberi.

CHAPTER 12

DEATH'S LONG SLEEP

As blood continues to spread across the land from a mad man's quest for power. We again bear witness to the warped mind and actions of the self-proclaimed king.

"Am I surrounded by incompetent fools or inept dogs?" Sammiel shouts. Bone-chilling fear grips the messengers who have the unfortunate task of reporting the loss of two divisions lost to Queen Aminatu and her people and a scouting party west of the encampment. They report that all warriors were lost at both sites, with no discernible tracks to follow except for those from the west. They tell of how they tracked a band of people to a body of water and the trail vanishes from that point on. Having received the news, Sammiel shockingly is calm. He gives thanks to the men and moves to a small chest nestled among his confiscated bounty. The assembled group of commanders, as well as the messengers, all brace for yet another outburst. For just to the right of bounty is a favorite sword of Sammiel's. It is the very sword that beheaded Onkala. But that is not to be. Sammiel calmly places the chest upon his table and opens it. He removes two pouches and tosses them to the two scouts. He politely dismisses them both. Just as they were about to exit Sammiel's quarters, they are halted by a question from Sammiel. "Could you determine how long it has been since these warriors' demise?" he asks.

"A little more than a week, Lord Sammiel," answers one of the scouts.

"I see," replies Sammiel, as he approaches the men. "Is that the situation for both areas, or did you conspire to lie to avoid the same fate as your brothers?" Sammiel asks.

"No, my lord," both men reply. A long silence and a murderous glare are Sammiel's response to their answer. "Go," he orders.

The men exit the quarters, Sammiel rejoins the commanders at his table. Once seated, he calmly says, "Let those two be examples of what is to come to those who do not give their all." The air is thick with tension, but all commanders bow in acceptance of the order. In turn, Sammiel asks, "Of whose command did these divisions belong?"

"That would be commander Askia, my Lord," someone utters. "He accompanied his men in the battle with the nomads."

"He died with his men in battle," proudly boasts Sammiel. "A great example of what is required to maintain dominance over these hostile lands," he concludes. "Let us put an end to this charade of opposition," he says. Getting to the matter of war, Sammiel makes the determination to march a full-scale assault into the nomad's lands. That would mean approximately five thousand men. "It only stands to reason that the jackal's stronghold is near the vicinity of the massacre of our two divisions," Sammiel points out. "It is there that we march to," he says as he points to the crude drawing of the last known location of the nomad's latest victory. "The flat lands at the base of Mount Nyiragongo shall be the place that we crush the upstart desert dogs and I will finally claim my bride. Prepare the army for the march. And give the order that we will seek any to join our ranks. All of their people die, save for the queen. We will erase them from the face of this world," commands Sammiel.

The counsel disperses and there is immediate activity as the commanders proceed to prepare the army for all-out war. But the commanders withhold apprehensions of the state of their Lord Sammiel. Fear of death prevents them from openly discussing the matter. They know that Sammiel has a bevy of spies throughout his warriors. So, if a single whisper of doubt were to be brought to Sammiel's attention, death would surely be the outcome with no remorse. They press on with their preparations over the next few days.

Sammiel himself remains in constant seclusion inside his quarters, with distinct instructions to not be disturbed. A ritual that he has practiced prior to every battle. But at this juncture of his reign, Sammiel has become dependent upon his council with Manyara, but the manifestation of their interaction in the physical realm brings questions of Sammiel's sanity among his men. Yet Sammiel is oblivious to this fact. A fact that lends credence to the possibility that he is indeed not of sound mind. Manyara's council to her son is repetitive and maddening. Each time he converses with his mother, she councils the same directive, "Kill them all, take the queen and end the bloodline!" In the end, Sammiel succumbs to the madness and screams out in anguish. The posted guards and all within earshot tremble with fear, but none dare enter Sammiel's chambers. That is the atmosphere that the men work within and many do not look forward to the day of the long march.

It has been six days since the union of forces. In that time, Zuberi has come to respect and admire King Numair. Numair has offered to have the men under Zuberi's command participate in training sessions, a gesture which Zuberi accepts and himself attends. In turn, Zuberi extends an offer to join his men on patrols to Numair. Numair sees an opportunity to discover and learn of new territories. He is more than willing to join the patrols and takes a small group of Menokang along. It was on one particular excursion that Numair first detected that something was amiss. With his heightened senses, the air smell and taste hide minute changes unnoticed by the average person. He also noticed that the wildlife would flock in large groups as if to suggest a migration. Odd for this time of season. Numair took notice, but could not exactly deduce the reason for these strange events.

That is, until one particular afternoon. Queen Aminatu has asked King Numair to accompany her. By now, the innocent fondness between the two has blossomed into a full-on romance. The pair have asked for privacy as they leave the encampment. A reluctant Zuberi does not render an argument of any consequence, as he now is confident in Numair's abilities. But he has yet to comprehend the full extent of the young king's power. As the couple starts their trip, Queen Aminatu tells Numair that she has a surprise for him and that it is the trust that has grown between the two that has given her his confidence. Numair smiles and coyly takes her hand in his. She freely accepts his strong touch. The trek takes the pair through the cave tunnel and through the waterfall. They are careful not to be exposed as they descend from the wall of rocks. Once on solid ground, they hasten the pace and make their way to the northwestern direction. An area that Numair has patrolled with the sentries on occasion, but today the route taken is altered. Aminatu leads him towards yet another hidden path. There, in a heavily vegetated area, is a rock formation like none Numair has seen. A garden of strange, black crystal-like rocks is their destination. At first glance, the rocks seem to grow from the soil around them. There are literally hundreds of smaller rocks covering the area leading up to the enormous rock crystals. But Aminatu simply turns to Numair and smiles as she leads him through a maze of the rock crystals. It turns out that in the rear of the garden is a path that is hidden by the boulders and camouflaged by the trees that are abundant. That the queen is comfortable enough to share this with him, entices his emotions. Finally, they reach the end of the climb onto a perch-like plateau. As Numair emerges, he is in awe! There before his very eyes is what could be the world, sprawled out as though the land blended with the heavens and beyond.

The beautiful site reveals majestic Mount Nyiragongo, beautiful hills and valleys, luscious green ranges, arid and dry deserts, large bodies of water, multiple rivers that resemble spiny fingers massaging the landscape. Aminatu proudly tells Numair, "This is one of the keys to the success of our people. We come to this location to plot our courses and to spy intruder marches upon our lands." With the evening sun lowering itself along the horizon, the couple admires the sparkle from the different water sources as they shimmer from the sun's setting rays.

"Thank you for sharing in something so beautiful and sacred to your people," says Numair. "It is spectacular!"

"I wanted to share something dear to my heart with you," says the now sun-kissed queen as the setting sun highlighted her. She gazes into Numair's eyes and she takes a chance. As Numair is admiring the breathtaking view, she suddenly kisses the naïve king. Numair pulls back for a second out of shock or embarrassment. Whatever the cause, now the queen becomes embarrassed and begins to apologize. But before she can utter her apology, King Numair takes her into his embrace, careful not to harm her, and gives her a long and passionate kiss. As they kiss, Aminatu throws both of her arms around Numair's neck and gives in to his strong embrace. As her body goes limp, Numair breaks the kiss momentarily.

"I have longed to do that from the moment I was first blessed to look upon you," he tells her.

"And I have waited for you to do that from the moment you first entered my quarters." And they kiss again.

Their romantic moment is interrupted as Numair's heightened senses again detect something in the air.

"What is wrong, my king?" asks Aminatu.

He replies that he does not know, there is something that has been in the air for a few days now. The two survey the land beneath them and see that birds are leaving the landscape in unusually large numbers. There is a smell that he has detected previously while on patrol with Aminatu's men, he tells her. But at that time it was faint but distinct. Today the odor is discernible and foul. With his acute senses on full alert, Numair begins to ask Aminatu questions about the landscape. It is here that he becomes aware of a not-too-distant volcano. A phenomenon that Numair and his people have never been exposed to. He only listens to her, but his mind is formulating possibilities.

Aminatu replies, "Perhaps it is some carcass of a slain animal that you detect."

Numair has experienced dead game before and none have ever given off such a foul odor as this.

"I do not know what it could be," responds Aminatu, "but come now. I have told you that I have a surprise for you and I have yet to give it to you," she says. Joyfully reaching into her side pouch. The queen removes Numair's hand coverings from his outfit that Kang made for him. Aminatu is all aglow as she hands them to Numair.

"How have you come to acquire my things?" asks Numair with a smile.

"From your mother," replies Aminatu. "I told her that I wanted to give you a gift and that I wanted one of your weapons to aid in the surprise, so she gave me these."

As Numair inspects and takes the gloves, he cannot help but notice that they have some added weight. As he unfurls them, there he finds on the fingers of the gloves what the extra weight is. It is the same strange shiny metal from the weapons that warriors use. The same metal that Bongani and his men brandished with their frail-looking weapons. And it is also the same metal that adorns Queen Aminatu's armaments. Aminatu is awash with glee.

"Try them on," she urges Numair. Numair is hesitant to do so. He chooses instead to lead Aminatu to a large boulder.

"You have shared a great many things today," he tells her. "So let me now share with you." With that Numair effortlessly punches a huge portion from the boulder. Aminatu is astounded!

"How is that possible?" she stutters, as she rushes to inspect Numair's hand.

Numair places a hand upon her soft and supple shoulder and looks into her eyes. "That is the gift of the prophecy for my people," he tells her. "I have the power of one hundred men, the senses of a wild beast, and the vision of a stealthy big cat hunter. And a host of other abilities." Aminatu, although shaken, immediately insists that Numair don the gloves now!

Numair openly displays his disbelief in the gift, yet he dons the gloves. "Now I want you to go to the same boulder," she instructs. "Only this time, I want you to claw it."

Numair immediately looks at her as though she is seeking amusement.

"Go on," she urges him.

Reluctantly Numair turns to the task at hand. With a mighty strike… crack! The boulder splits into several pieces. Numair is dumbfounded.

"How, how is that possible?" he now asks.

Aminatu is beside herself with laughter. "That is the result of a metal vigorously melted down and fitted to your gloves."

"What is this metal you speak of?" inquires Numair.

"We really do not know, but my grandfather found a very limited deposit of it many years ago. Through time we have learned to manipulate it and shape it to suit our needs. It is impervious to penetration or damage. I had been told of your fighting skills and wanted to enhance your advantage in battle, but never would I have imagined the depth of your abilities. This assures that your enemies will fall in defeat regardless of who they may be."

"I have but one enemy that will fall and..." suddenly Numair stops and begins to survey the area. He walks to the edge of the plateau and back. "We must leave now," he says. "Dusk will soon be upon us."

She agrees, but not until they again embrace in a long passionate kiss. Then they descend back down through the path. As they are exiting the black crystal garden, Numair once again takes notice of the strange crystals. The couple now playfully run back along the trail. Occasionally Numair takes Aminatu into his arms and carries her. He boastfully exhibits his incredible speed. The two enter the encampment as royals, but the ruse deceives no one. Particularly the other women in Numair's life.

Numair then turns to Aminatu and asks for her to call for an immediate council meeting. Trusting in Numair, she summons Zuberi and instructs him to dispatch messengers to the allied tribes. While in wait, Numair speaks to those present.

"We must march upon Sammiel now," he begins. All clamor for an explanation. Numair is calm and poised as he announces, "If we do not, we shall all surely die!" A stunned silence falls upon everyone. Numair, now with the setting sunlight at his back, studies his audience. He understands their fears, hesitations and even hatred. But it his steely resolve that he brings to order the group. Sammiel is drunk with power. He is guided in thinking that he is favored by the gods and has no threats. He has spread his forces out of range in order to capture more lands, people and stolen riches.

He may be aware of our presence. But he is unaware of our tactics and skills. They fight with sheer brute force. Whereas we are organized and strike with precision. If we allow him and his forces to gather, we can be over-run and annihilated. If we are to free our lands of this scourge, we must suffocate Sammiel and his minimal forces with haste! There is a stunned silence among the group now. But an unspoken understanding that the man, no the king before them has determined their task. And with a stoic stare around the room and into the faces of his comrades that they can now see the spark of hope and confidence in his eyes and all accept what must come about.

With their goals in place, the gathered begin to plan for the upcoming confrontation. With their spirits reinforced by the tenacity of the king and his compassion for his people. The night air is refreshing and the sounds from the land flow in harmony with the calm of Numair. He in solitude, gazing up to the heavens. In the distance he hears the roars of the big cats of the land vanquishing an opponent. The sounds fortifies his resolve. And he draws upon the wisdom of the ancestors for what must be done to ensure victory in the coming days. The stage is set and purpose is clear. Sammiel and his legions will be destroyed!